Fallen

By

A.J. Messenger

First Print Edition August 2016

ISBN-13: 978-1537069845

ISBN-10: 1537069845

Cover images credit:

Leigh Prather | Dreamstime.com

Artindustry | Dreamstime.com

Books by A.J. Messenger

The Guardian Series

Guardian (book one)

Fallen (book two)

Revelation (book three)

Learn more about new releases and contact me

I welcome you to visit me and subscribe to my newsletter to be the first to know about upcoming releases.

 ajmessenger.com

 facebook.com/ajmessengerauthor

 @aj_messenger

Dedication

Thank you to my family, whom I love and whom I can always count on for support in all my endeavors, and a warm thank you to all the readers who took a moment from their busy lives to write and say how much they loved *Guardian*.

"A candle that lights another candle loses nothing and spreads more light to the world."

Table of Contents

*"Physical science [progresses by] discovering
what sorts of things can be precisely explained.
These may be fewer than we thought."*

– Steven Weinberg, Nobel Prize Winning Physicist

*"And yet for all this help of head and brain
How happily instinctive we remain,
Our best guide upward further to the light,
Passionate preference such as love at sight."*

– Robert Frost

Preface

I'm melting into the sea.

I'm folding into a warm, welcoming blanket that I want to immerse myself in fully so I can stop this endless effort, endless struggle, getting nowhere.

Why fight the inevitable?

This is how it ends. No more pain. No more worry. Wherever Alexander is, he won't have to put himself in danger for me anymore.

Gradually I cease swaying my arms and legs in the waves and let my body flow beneath the sea, drifting downward, ever deeper … quietly and peacefully … into the abyss.

Avestan has finally won.

Chapter One

"What if I jump off a cliff?"

"What?" Alexander squints at me strangely, shielding his eyes from the sun with his hand.

We're sitting on our surfboards out in the ocean during a lull between wave sets. I've never been great at surfing but I love the combination of peaceful, meditative swaying punctuated by thrilling, adrenaline-pumping exhilaration. And it's a great workout—I'm always exhausted afterwards. I get why Alexander likes it so much.

I smooth away the lock of hair that has dipped in front of my right eye and tuck it behind my ear for the hundredth time. *Note to self: never cut your own bangs. No matter how good they look on Liz.* "You're going to stay as you are now," I say, "as an angel, forever. And I'm going to keep growing older. But what if I jump off a cliff? Or get eaten by a shark? Right now? Then I'd stay this age always."

His eyes meet mine for a long, slow stare. I can't quite pinpoint his expression but from the slight turn at the corner of his mouth I think he's going to humor me. "Okay, for the sake of convoluted arguments, let's say you *did* jump off a cliff—"

"Or got eaten by a shark."

"She says nonchalantly as we sit in the middle of the ocean on surfboards the size and shape of seals." His delivery is dry and his eyes flash bewilderment, or perhaps amusement.

"As if saying it will make it happen?"

"What you focus on ..."

I squint at him. "Is that really true?"

"Not always directly. But what you choose to give your attention to—or not—can shift the energy around you."

I consider his answer. "Well it's not as if you'd let anything happen to me."

"No," he says with a smile as he leans over and gently tucks my errant hair in place again, "but I'm enjoying the peace out here in the water with you and I don't particularly feel like fighting off a shark today."

I laugh. "Okay. I jump off a cliff then."

"You're forgetting the fact that you would die."

"You said energy never dies."

"Okay," he smiles, "you'd transform."

"Right … I'd transform into a guardian and then you and I would be together as guardians forever. You said my aura showed I was about to be realized."

He shakes his head. "You can't become a guardian that way. *Intent* matters. And there are no guarantees about anything, including becoming a guardian."

"So there's no way around it."

"Even if it was possible," he says, "you know you could never do that to your mom. Or Finn and Liz. And I wouldn't let you."

"I know," I concede. He's right. I would never leave them that way. "I doubt I'm going to become a guardian anyway," I add.

"Why?"

"Wouldn't I know it if I was? Wouldn't I feel especially wise … or *ready* in some way? My whole life I've felt like I don't know what the heck I'm doing from one moment to the next. How could I go from that to being a guardian?"

A smile reaches Alexander's deep green eyes. "Declan, it's the people who think they know it all that have the most to learn."

"Well," I say, considering his words, "that may be, but I haven't done anything particularly important."

"What's important? You see people for who they are and you understand the connection we all share—that's a rare quality." He pauses before continuing. "But I understand how you feel. When I look back, most of what I did throughout most of my lives doesn't seem spectacularly grand."

"What do you mean?"

"I wonder sometimes how I came to be a guardian."

"You do? But you were good."

"Yes," he nods, "and you're good, too, day after day, in big ways and small that ripple out with consequences you'll never realize."

"And that's enough?"

"Apparently," he says with a smile as he spreads his arms wide, "since I'm sitting here now as your guardian."

I smile, shading my eyes from the sun. "I hope you're right."

His expression turns thoughtful. "It's about doing the right thing, when it's not easy. And it's about cycles and learning more each time. But I've wondered if my being realized was more about the way my life ended."

"You mean because you tried to save Alenna from Avestan?"

"More like something to do with lives being taken so abruptly—with fear … and violence. I don't know," he says, his voice drifting off, "I used to wonder if becoming a guardian was a way to bring peace and maybe I wasn't truly worthy. I took my brother's life, after all."

"You were trying to save a life."

Alexander looks down at his surfboard, not saying anything.

"I understand," I say softly.

He looks back up and meets my eyes.

"I can imagine how that must hurt," I say, "with the way things ended."

Alexander holds my gaze for a long beat and in my mind I try to imagine the shock and horror of being murdered by your own brother and being forced to stab him back as you try to save someone you love. The rage Avestan must have been consumed with—to kill Alexander and Alenna with a knife, up close and personal. I look at the jagged scar Alexander keeps on his left temple as a reminder and my heart hurts for the memories he must hold of his last mortal life.

"I've never actually voiced these thoughts aloud," he says.

I meet his eyes. "You saved me from Avestan … against every odd and obstacle. If that doesn't prove you were meant to be a guardian I don't know what would."

"We saved each other," he says quietly. "But you're right—when I'm with you I feel as if I'm where I'm supposed to be. And Edwin always says certainty is for idiots."

"That sounds pretty informal for Edwin."

He smiles. "Okay, what he actually says is 'To pursue truth we must doubt all things as much as possible.' In other words, only those fooling themselves are cocksure."

My eyebrow rises. "Is that an Australian thing?"

"What?"

"Cocksure."

"What do you mean?"

"I want to know if I should add it to my list of favorite words you use, like jaffle or tosser."

He chuckles. "It's just a word. It means arrogantly confident."

"I know what it means, silly. It's just not heard much in everyday conversation."

"To society's detriment," he says with a wry smile.

I laugh and I find myself surveying his kind eyes and warm smile and marveling at this angel before me. How I love the way Alexander sounds, from the timbre of his voice to his accent to the odd words he sometimes tosses out. He's so different and I love that. Even if he wasn't an angel he'd still seem otherworldly to me.

"Well," I say, forcing myself to focus back on our conversation, "I think it's a mark of your intelligence and worthiness that you're not cocksure. The very fact that you've questioned if you were meant to be a guardian means you were meant to be one."

He smiles.

"And any lingering doubts keep you striving that much harder to do good," I add.

His smile reaches his eyes and they crinkle handsomely. "Have I told you how much I love sprites?" he says. "Especially smart sprites that embrace doubt and mock my vocabulary?"

I laugh. "Well I have a long, sordid history of doubting myself. So if doubt can serve a good purpose for once, I'm all for embracing it."

He holds my gaze for a long beat and then his eyes trace a path around my face. "Your aura is beautiful right now," he says softly. "It's shimmering brilliantly with vivid whites and rich blues ... it's hard to tell where you end and the ocean and the sky begins. I never get tired of looking at you."

Our eyes meet and the air around us is charged with electric energy. Combined with the quiet sounds of the water lapping and the soft undulation of the swells, I feel as if there's no place in the world I belong other than right here, right now, in this moment with Alexander. I take a deep breath and surrender into the sensation as he holds my gaze.

"Do you feel this right now?" he asks. "Between us? How our auras blend? You don't have to come up with crazy ideas like jumping off cliffs. This feeling we have when we're together makes age meaningless."

I nod. "I know you're right," I say, looking down. "I guess I just like the idea of growing old together ..."

"Like that couple we always see holding hands as they walk on the beach," he says. "I understand."

I meet his eyes, surprised. "Yes ... I don't know why it matters so much. Maybe it's because my mom and dad didn't get to ... I look at pictures of us with my dad sometimes ... it's been almost ten years now ... my mom and I keep getting older but my dad is frozen in time. Like we're leaving him behind."

Alexander leans over and takes my hand. "You haven't left him. He's still around. Somewhere. Everywhere."

"Why don't I feel him then?" I ask.

"Would it make you feel better to know that someday you could all be together again?"

"You said there are no guarantees. For any of us."

"There aren't, but there are some things I *know*. Things that are right with the universe. And you and I are one. I know, in every thrumming part of my being, that we were meant to find each other. The way our energy connects … it's a kind of harmony I've never felt before."

I close my eyes for a moment to focus on the feeling. "It's like we're on the same frequency," I say softly before I open my eyes again.

"Yes," he says with a smile. "Some energies belong together, and from everything you've told me your mum and dad had a deep love between them. When you have a powerful soul connection like that you tend to find each other over and over across lifetimes."

I nod. The idea of them together again, in a future life, does make me feel better. And it feels right. Maybe I could find them, too. The thought makes me smile.

Alexander leans over and kisses me softly. "I love you," he says.

"I love you, too," I say and my heart swells with the truth of it.

"Should we head back?" he asks as he looks around. "I think the waves are all rubbish now."

I nod. "I can't feel my feet anyway."

"Told you you should have worn booties."

"I like the way the board feels under my feet," I say as I swing my legs out of the water and lie on my chest so I can start paddling.

"Aye, but if you can't feel your feet, you can't feel the board."

I splash water in his direction. "Don't spoil my argument with logic."

He laughs. "Give me your foot." He eases his board alongside mine and places his hands around my foot. Immediately it feels enveloped in soothing heat.

"*Ohhh,* that feels so good," I groan. "Where were you an hour ago?"

He smiles. "You do the other one."

"How?"

"Imagine your light sending warmth to your foot."

"I can do that?"

"Only one way to find out," he says with a shrug. "Didn't you say you felt warm when you used your energy before?"

He's right. It's worth a try. I close my eyes and conjure a ball of white light in my core. I imagine it growing brighter and spreading out to my limbs and then rolling over to my right foot. Very slowly, as I focus and concentrate, I feel my foot thawing from within, getting warmer as the white light unfurls from my heel to my toes. It's not as hot and as fast as when Alexander warmed my other foot but *I'm doing it myself.* "It's working," I say with amazement as I open my eyes and look at Alexander.

"One more sprite power you can add to the list," he says.

"Ability to warm feet while surfing. Check," I say. "That'll scare the pants off the dark angels."

Alexander bursts out laughing. "I think you're far more powerful than you realize," he says as I bask in the warmth of my newly-toasty feet and we paddle happily towards shore.

We strip off our wetsuits when we reach the sand and sit back on our elbows on our towels to soak up the warm summer rays. I'm wearing a bright yellow bikini and Alexander has on a pair of blue and yellow Billabong board shorts that hang low on his hips. His ab muscles ripple as he rolls himself up to unzip his backpack and extract two Capri Suns.

"Do you remember the first time we had these together?" he asks as he sits back and hands one to me.

"Up on the mountain when you took me flying for the first time," I say with a grin. "On Valentine's Day."

He nods and meets my eyes. "I wanted to kiss you that day."

"Is that right?"

He nods again. "Very badly." His voice is low and husky.

I smile, besotted, and my eyes trail to his kissable lips as that familiar electric charge hangs in the air between us.

"If only I'd known I could have come close like this," he says as he leans over until we're a breath away. "And I could have kissed you, like this," he says as he grazes my lips, softly at first, and then harder as the kiss deepens.

We lie back on the towel and I melt into the sensation, my arms around his muscled frame as his lips part mine, our tongues teasing and exploring. He groans, deep within his throat, as our bodies entwine and I sigh softly, but before long Alexander pulls back and lies down on the towel beside me. He closes his eyes and rakes his fingers through his dark, tousled hair, letting out a long, slow breath as he faces up to the sky. "We should probably get going soon," he says finally.

I steady my own breath and peer around at the emptiness in all directions. "Why?"

He turns on his side to face me and I do the same.

"Because everything else falls away when I'm with you," he says with an intensity in his eyes that makes my breath hitch in my throat.

"And?"

"And," he smiles, "I'm still getting used to the idea that we can do this." He leans over and kisses me again softly.

"You're getting used to it?" I say.

He nods, slowly. "Yes … I'm getting used to the fact that I can kiss you here …" he says as he kisses one eyelid softly. "And right here …" he says as he kisses the other eyelid. "And over here …" he murmurs as he trails kisses along my cheek and over to my ear where I feel his breath hot on my skin. "But especially here …" he says as he makes his way back to my mouth and kisses me with an ardor that makes me sigh.

"I love it when you sigh like that," he groans.

I smile against his lips as I kiss him back.

The invisible string between us glows and embraces my heart with a warm, white light that crowds out the worries in the back of my mind—about how Alexander and I can be together long term, or when Avestan will be back and how he'll seek his vengeance against us.

When we finally sit up to watch the sun set with our arms wrapped around one another, I rest my head on Alexander's shoulder.

He holds me close and kisses the top of my head softly before he asks a question I've been avoiding for far too long.

"Declan, do you want to talk about what happened to your dad?"

Chapter Two

"You said it was some kind of accident? But I understand if you don't want to talk about it," Alexander says softly.

I shake my head. It's not as if it's some big secret. I assumed he would have asked someone else by now or researched it online, but Alexander being Alexander he obviously respected my privacy and waited until I was ready to share it with him personally.

"It's okay," I say quietly. "I can talk about it."

"You want to go somewhere else first? Are you getting cold?"

"No, I like being out here with you."

I study a strip of billowy marshmallow clouds on the horizon with fiery light shining at their edges as the sun falls behind them. The sky is shot through with vibrant pink and orange hues and the effect over the water is brilliantly gorgeous. On days like today, even before I met Alexander, I would have believed that there are angels in the world all around us. He hugs me close as we sit, and the rhythmic, soothing beat of his heart makes me feel eminently safe. Eventually I look up into his eyes before I begin.

"I think I told you my dad was a partner at Fields and Morris, the big law firm in town. You saw Burt Fields once when he came to our house. Or he may have left before you arrived ... anyway, he was my dad's best friend. He started the firm."

Alexander nods.

"They used to have an annual trip for the partners every summer. They would go out on the firm's yacht and spend the weekend at sea. It was supposed to be an off-site meeting and fishing trip but mostly it was about taking a break and having fun according to my dad. He always had a good time. My mom used to say he brought the sun into any room or party …"

Alexander smiles and his kind eyes soften the pain in my heart.

"That was the last time I saw him," I continue, "right before he went on that trip." My voice cracks a little before I can finish and Alexander takes my hands in his.

"What happened?" he asks softly.

"No one knows exactly," I say as I wipe away tears. "Burt said everyone had been drinking and he must have fallen off the boat … maybe hit his head so he couldn't call for help. It was dark, at night."

"Did your dad drink a lot?" asks Alexander.

"No," I say. "My mom says he hardly drank at all. So that never made any sense. Somebody even speculated that maybe he jumped on purpose. That was the most hurtful. Burt told my mom he'd never forgive himself for not noticing sooner that my dad was missing. He had a hard time dealing with it for a long while afterwards. We all did, but I think Burt blamed himself."

"Did your dad seem depressed?"

"No. I remember my mom saying he was a little preoccupied with a case at the time but we had a big vacation planned and he was looking forward to so many things. My dad would never leave us on purpose. I know that in my heart."

"Did they do an autopsy?"

I shake my head and wipe my fingers under my eyes to clear away more tears. "They never found him. 'Lost at sea' was how they described it on the news. There was a search for a while but eventually they had to give up."

Alexander pulls me into an embrace and I feel him kiss the top of my head as he strokes my hair with his hand. "I'm so sorry, Declan."

I rest my head on his chest and enjoy the warm safety of his arms wrapped around me. "Next week is the anniversary. My mom and I always walk to the ocean every year to talk to him. When I run here in the mornings I sometimes talk to him then, too, as I look out over the water."

"What do you say?"

"I tell him how much I miss him. And I ask for some sign that he's okay ... I just want to know that he's all right, you know?" I look up at Alexander with watery eyes and he nods.

"We used to go on long walks together," I say quietly. "I miss those the most."

Alexander caresses my cheek and wipes away a tear with his thumb. "Do you ever tell him about your life?"

I nod. "Sometimes. I told him about you," I say with a smile. "And I told him about Liz and Finn getting together—I know he'd get a kick out of that." I laugh softly. "He would love Liz. She gets Finn the same way my dad did."

Alexander smiles.

"Mostly I tell him how much I wish he was here."

"He's not gone," says Alexander. "His energy continues."

"I know ... but it's not the same."

"Have you ever felt his presence?"

"What do you mean?"

"Like you saw something or the wind blew a certain way at the right moment?"

"Maybe ... but isn't that just wishful thinking?" I ask. "He used to help me with my anxiety, and I counted on the fact that if he was really around he would have continued to help me figure it out instead of letting me suffer all those years until you came along."

"Maybe I was the help."

My heart begins to pound as what Alexander said sinks in. "Are you saying my dad sent you?"

"No," he says immediately, "no, no, Declan. I'm sorry, I didn't mean to give that impression. I would have told you if I knew your dad. But energy can work indirectly. Has there ever been anything that made you wonder if he was communicating with you?"

"There was one thing," I say, my mind drifting back to a dusty memory. "But it was only right after he died ... I was having a hard time and my mom suggested we write letters and send them to my dad so I could feel like I had some control again. I wrote him a long letter telling him how much I missed him and my mom did the same and we folded them up and stuck them in two balloons—sky blue because that was his favorite color. Then we filled the balloons with helium and tied them off and went to the beach to let them go. It made me feel like I could talk to him again and he wasn't really gone, just somewhere else."

Alexander nods.

"That night I dreamt about my dad," I continue. "He came to the house and I supposed we were getting ready for a party because he was carrying three balloons: two sky-blue and one purple. At first it all felt normal but slowly I started to remember that my dad was gone and none of this could be real. But I was overwhelmed with happiness that he was there and I started to cry and I told him how much I missed him, and he began to flicker and fade and he told me he loved me and he was sorry but he couldn't stay." Tears well up in my eyes as I remember the dream vividly.

"The next day I told my mom about the dream and she called Finn's mom."

"Why?"

"My dad and Finn had this special bond. So Finn was hurting ... and he saw me hurting, and I think he didn't know what to do with all those emotions. He was pacing a lot and tapping his chest and eating crazy stuff like hot peppers and his mom was worried. He had this blue blanket he would never take off his shoulders whenever he was home. I think he felt helpless, like I did. So my mom told Mrs. Cooper about the balloon idea and she wanted to find out if they'd done it already."

"Had they?" he asks.

I nod. "And my mom asked what color balloon Finn used." I pause and look up into Alexander's eyes. "I could tell what Mrs. Cooper's answer was by the look on my mom's face."

"Purple."

"That felt real to me," I say with a nod, full of emotion. "Like my dad got our messages."

Alexander hugs me closer.

"Right?" I ask as I swallow the tender lump in my throat.

"Strong emotions draw energy together. And love is the most powerful of all."

My eyes well up as I nod. "That's what I thought."

"The funny thing is," I add with a choked-up laugh, "when I tried to tell Finn about it he wouldn't listen. He told me, 'It's universal that no one wants to hear anyone's dreams.'"

Alexander laughs as he wraps his arms around me tighter and I feel his energy fill the space around us as we watch the summer sun complete its descent, infusing the sky with color in every direction.

In my mind, as the waves lap gently against the shore, I whisper to my dad how very much I love him, and how much I wish he was still here.

Chapter Three

"Alright lovebirds, break it up," says Liz as she walks up to us in the back parking lot outside Jack's Burger Shack. Alexander came to meet me on my break from work and we just finished having lunch. Okay, in that exact moment we were kissing, to be more precise. All those months it was forbidden and now I guess we're making up for lost time. I'd kiss him all day if I could.

"Come over tonight," Liz says. "My parents are gone for the weekend and Finn's making dinner."

My eyes widen.

"It's okay," she says with a laugh. "Seriously. I'm teaching him how to cook."

I peer over at Alexander and he smiles. "We're in," he says in that easy way of his.

It's been only two weeks since our graduation from San Mar High, yet I feel remarkably more grown up. Something tells me that this summer, before college starts, may be the most carefree I'll ever be. Sure, I'm working like crazy, but there's no schoolwork to worry about and somehow I have more spare time combined with more delicious freedom than ever before. Yes, Avestan weighs heavily in the back of my mind, but I'm determined to live in the moment while also preparing for his return (well, as much as anyone can prepare, I guess, for a dark angel's angry resurgence).

The summer break isn't all I'm excited about, though. By some turn of fate Finn, Liz and I will all be going to the same place in the fall, here in San Mar. Finn got into every school he applied to but he decided on UCSM in the end because of their space sciences program. Liz didn't get accepted into

Stanford, as she hoped, but UCSM was a close second choice. I managed to win an academic scholarship to UCSM and when you combine it with my savings, the money I earn from working, and the money I'm saving by living at home, I think I can pull it off. Alexander, of course, will be there, too and Edwin's visiting professorship is now open-ended.

"What can we bring?" I ask Liz.

"How about a pizza in case Finn blows up the kitchen?" she replies before she breaks into a smile. "Just kidding! I'm sure it'll be fine … most likely. Come over around eight." She turns to yank open the back door. "I better clock in now," she says as she heads in, "or Jack will be even more ticked off that I forgot to wear my 'Home of the Hula Burger' t-shirt. Again."

I laugh and glance over at Alexander after she goes inside. "She hates that shirt," I say. Then I peek at the time on my watch. "My break's over, I'd better go inside, too."

"I need to go, anyway," Alexander says as we stand up from the picnic table. "Edwin and I have a meeting to go to."

"One of your 'once a fortnight' angel meetings?" I ask.

He smiles. "Saving the world from dark forces requires some administrative planning."

I laugh as he walks me to the back door with his arm around me and turns to face me before I go in. "Are we taking our lives in our hands?" he asks.

"What?"

"Eating food prepared by Finn."

I laugh. "You're immortal, what do you have to worry about?"

"Maybe I'm worried about the rest of you," he smiles. "Finn told me he nearly burned down his parent's house once when he left the toaster oven on."

"He's exaggerating," I say with a dismissive wave of my hand. "A small fire damaged one cupboard and the poor guy never forgave himself. Honestly, the worst outcome we're probably facing is either boxed macaroni and cheese or some recipe Liz foists on him that Finn meticulously measures and prepares only to throw in the oven and forget to ever take it out. He *hates* cooking. I don't know what Liz is thinking."

Alexander laughs. "I love you," he says as he gives me a kiss. "But seriously, should we bring take-away in case this goes south?"

I smile. "Nah, Plan B is, we hit Rico's afterwards."

"I met some guy today who knows you," Liz says as we sit at the large table in her kitchen, ready to eat. She's scooping veggie lasagna onto our plates. I'm surprised to note that not only is the lasagna *not* burned to a crisp, it smells delicious.

"Did you really make this, Finn?" I ask. "It looks seriously good."

"I made it," says Finn dryly. "But I didn't enjoy it."

Alexander and I laugh.

"We agreed that once a month we'd both try something new for each other," Liz explains. "Like software upgrades on ourselves."

"Making this lasagna is worth at least three months," says Finn.

"Well, that book series you want me to read is worth three *years*," Liz retorts. "They have a million pages each."

"The longest one is 987 pages," replies Finn. "I read them all in 12 days."

Liz groans. "I don't understand why you care if I read them."

Finn looks up. "I want you to read them so I can talk with you about them."

"Haven't you already talked them to death with your book club?" she asks.

"No," he says. "I want your perspective. You bring up ideas I never would have considered. I like hearing what you have to say. You're interesting and it'll make me like the books more." The sincerity in his voice as he meets Liz's gaze makes my heart literally warm in my chest.

I peer over and can see that Liz's heart has officially melted too. "All right," she says. "I want to read them now."

Finn smiles. "Thanks," he replies. "I think this is resolved."

I laugh to myself. I imagine Finn with a ledger in his head of outstanding issues that he checks off as either "resolved" or "unresolved/pending." He craves equilibrium and appreciates pleasant outcomes.

Liz leans over and plants a kiss on him. He's probably the only guy in the world that could make fiery Liz so agreeable and he does it without even trying. In fact, that's probably the key—it works because he's so honest and completely devoid of manipulation.

"So, anyway," Liz says, now all smiles, "getting back to our original conversation … after you left today, this guy came into Jack's and he made me promise I'd tell you he said hello. It was kinda weird …"

"Who was he?" I ask as I pass the salad bowl to Finn.

"He was good looking, but in a creepy sort of way if that makes sense. Said he knew you through Molly Bing … which I found very odd. Why would you know Molly's boyfriend?"

My heart freezes in my chest. "What was his name?" I ask as I swallow hard and exchange a glance with Alexander.

"Actually, I think he's her ex-boyfriend," continues Liz, "they used to go out was what he said … oh what the hell was his name—it was something like Avatar or Ava-something-or-other. Does that sound familiar?"

My heart begins to pound so hard I fear it's going to beat a hole through my chest. I feel like I've been jolted back in time to when anxiety like this plagued me on a daily basis. Alexander squeezes my hand under the table and I can feel him flooding me with calm, soothing energy. I center myself and do the same. I can't give into panic.

"What exactly did he say?" Alexander asks Liz, his voice steady and reassuring.

"He just said to tell Declan he's back in town and he'll be seeing her soon. The way he said it made the hairs on the back of my neck stand up … which I suppose is how I would react to any guy who would date Queen B. Although I have to say he's better looking than her typical jock boyfriends. I didn't know she went for the hot, dangerous type. Although I'm sure he's just as stup—"

"Stay away from him," says Alexander sharply.

"Why?" asks Liz, looking surprised. "You know him?"

"His name is Avestan," I say. "I had a run-in with him once when I was babysitting Charlie Bing. He's not a good guy. Please don't talk to him or go near him if you see him again."

I look over at Finn. "I mean that for you, too. Stay away from Avestan, okay, Finn?"

"I have no idea who you're talking about," he replies. He's tucked into his lasagna and not paying attention.

"I have a picture of him," I say as I start to reach for my purse but I remember that the photo I took on my phone turned black, disturbing me greatly. "Actually, I forgot, I don't have it anymore."

Liz looks at me for a long time, studying my expression. "He's a pretty recognizable guy … I'll point him out to Finn if he comes around," she reassures me, her voice serious now. "But you owe me more of an explanation on this later."

I nod and I'm grateful when Alexander changes the subject. "I heard you and Edwin had a nice discussion the other day," he says to Finn.

Finn nods. "It must be nice living with him so you can discuss theories about space and time whenever you want."

Alexander smiles and squeezes my hand under the table. "He's looking forward to you taking his class in September."

We finish our meal and after everyone helps clear the table and load the dishwasher, Liz and I stay back in the kitchen for a moment while Finn and Alexander go out on the deck to look at the stars through Liz's new telescope, a graduation present.

"So what's this idea about teaching Finn to cook?" I ask as we sit at the swivel bar stools lined up along the large, marble island in the middle of the expansive chef's kitchen. "You know he hates it."

"I thought it would be good for him to learn how to make a couple decent meals. Even a cute genius needs street skills."

I laugh. "Cooking is a street skill?"

"When the zombie apocalypse happens every skill counts."

I shake my head. "In that scenario, I think Finn would be one of the scientists working in a lab somewhere on a plan to wipe the zombies out."

"Maybe, but he'd need to eat while he's working."

"He'd be perfectly happy to survive on Cheez-its and peanut butter sandwiches."

She laughs. "Maybe so, but when all the Cheez-its and peanut butter are gone he needs a backup plan."

I smile. "Software upgrades, huh?"

"It was actually Finn's idea. He's on this self-betterment plan where he's setting yearly goals for himself."

"You mean like how he's learning Japanese?" I ask.

"Yeah, and he also decided he would only eat meat he slaughtered himself—which quickly morphed into becoming a vegetarian because he couldn't bring himself to kill any animals."

I smile. How Finn thought he'd be able to harm any living thing is the only surprise there.

"I suggested we also do mini-goals," Liz continues, "on a monthly basis, but focused on things for each other … which was really more of a ploy to get him to rub my feet after a shift at Jack's but it turned into a good idea."

I laugh. "What's your yearly goal?"

"I'm teaching myself to juggle. Oh, and meditate. Ten minutes a day. So I don't flip out at all the asshats who come into Jack's and keep changing their orders."

"Like Jordan Piner," we both chant in unison, cracking ourselves up.

"That guy is so stoned all the time," says Liz. "How did he even graduate?"

"He not only graduated, I heard he completed two years at Cabrina and he's headed to UCLA in the fall."

She raises an eyebrow. "Shit, really? Maybe being baked helps him concentrate." We contemplate that idea as we take a sip of our iced teas. "You guys want to watch a movie?" she asks.

"Thanks, but not tonight. I should probably get home. I haven't seen my mom in a while."

"I'm sure she appreciates the alone time."

"What? Why?"

"So Chief Stephens can go all Willy Wonka in her wonderland," Liz says with a jaunty smile.

"What the—? Jesus, Liz, that's the *last* mental picture I want in my mind … and *Willy Wonka?* C'mon," I wail, "I loved that movie!"

Liz laughs out loud. "Did I ever tell you about the time I walked in on my parents? They were here in the kitchen and my mom had these ice cubes and a spatula—"

"Oh my God," I cry out as I put my hands over my ears, "please stop talking—I'll never be able to eat in here ever again."

She throws her head back and laughs uproariously. "If I have to live with it, you do too! Share my pain, sister!"

I smile and shake my head. "You're seriously traumatizing me."

She laughs some more, unfazed.

"I'm glad my mom's finally dating a little," I say after a moment of thought, "but do you really think they're—"

"Of course," Liz says emphatically. "And that's a good thing. It's about time for good ol' Judy Jane."

I consider this for a moment. Then I promptly discount it. *Nah,* Liz is wrong. I mean I'm happy for my mom if she is, but I know how conflicted she's been about even agreeing to a date. I'm also conflicted, if I'm being honest. And, *yeesh,* the last thing I want to do is think about my mom's sex life, or Mr.

and Mrs. Warner's—in this kitchen—with a *spatula* for Christ's sake. I glance over at Liz and want to simultaneously laugh and burn the image out of my mind forever.

I peer out on the deck to see Alexander and Finn talking animatedly and pointing up at the night sky. "I still think I'll go home tonight and see my mom," I say. "I'm volunteering at the shelter in the morning and I want to get up early and run first. Plus, it'll give you and Finn some time alone."

I don't mention that the real reason I'm anxious to leave is because the last time I saw Avestan—before Alexander managed to nearly kill him and help us escape Nusquam—his eyes were trained on me with a malevolent evil so vicious it still haunts me in my sleep.

Now he's back in San Mar.

And there's no telling how he'll seek his revenge.

Chapter Four

"What are we going to do?" I ask as we drive away from Liz's house.

"We knew he'd be back," Alexander replies.

"But why would he approach Liz?"

"To frighten you."

I don't answer and Alexander reaches over and squeezes my hand. "He knew it would get to you. He's not going to harm Liz. Or anyone. The guardians won't let him," he says as he meets my eyes. "We've been expecting this. It's a good thing, in a way, that he's finally come out of hiding."

"A *good* thing?"

"No more waiting and wondering. Now we can move forward." He glances over at me. "Please don't worry."

"Why shouldn't I worry?"

He eases over to the side of the street and pulls to a stop in front of a random house in Liz's neighborhood of nicely appointed estates. Then he turns to me and takes my hands in his and looks into my eyes. "You don't need to worry because I have a plan."

"You always have a plan," I say, holding back a smile, "for everything."

He smiles crookedly. "I believe in being prepared."

"Were you a boy scout or something?"

"No," he chuckles. "I had a paper round, though. Does that count? It took a lot of planning to make my bike route efficient."

I smile and push his arm. "So what's the plan?" I ask, getting serious again.

"Well, the first step involves talking."

"Talking? You mean with your fists?"

"*What?* No," he laughs, shaking his head, "I think you've been watching too many kung fu movies."

I try not to smile. Finn and I do watch a lot of kung fu movies. Something about the stupid plots interspersed with cool fight scenes—all that confidence is mesmerizing. But this is serious.

"So you mean actual talking," I say.

"Yes, with words."

His manner is so nonchalant it's disconcerting. If he's acting this way so he won't frighten me it's actually having a paradoxical effect. "So, *diplomacy,*" I say with obvious skepticism, "with dark angels."

"Yes. Diplomacy can work—even with dark angels. They wear their human nature like a ball and chain. But that's not what our conversation will be focused on. I'll attempt an agreement—it'll be down to him to accept—but I expect it won't go anywhere. I'll be using our talk to extract information."

"What do you mean?"

"Everyone wants something. And it's usually not what they think they want. When someone wants something bad enough, it creates an opportunity."

"But the only thing Avestan wants is to destroy us," I say.

He shakes his head. "It's more than that now. This is about me and Avestan."

"I thought he wanted me for my aura?"

"He did. But now that we defeated him, it's about winning. Against me."

"What information are you trying to get?" I ask.

"Information that dark guardians are forbidden to reveal."

"So why would Avestan tell you?"

"Because at their base, dark angels are controlled by human nature."

"You keep saying that. Do you realize that's a little insulting to us human mortals? Or near mortals?"

He smiles. "Sorry. I should have said the worst sides of human nature. All I mean is that I'll use it to my advantage."

"That's all you're going to say?"

"Once it's sorted I'll share more. In the meantime, everyone's protected. I know you're worried about that, but please don't be. Finn and Liz and everyone else have had extra guardians around them for months. All of San Mar, in fact."

"Then how did Avestan get to Liz?"

"Protected doesn't mean sheltered. Guardians have to let mortals live their lives. And that includes interacting with dark angels. But Avestan knew he was being watched. And you heard Liz, her instincts are good. She kept her distance."

"I fell under Avestan's spell once. She could, too."

"You didn't believe enough in your instincts then. You're stronger now. And the way Avestan targeted you was irregular."

I meet his eyes. "What do you mean?"

"Dark angels don't usually pursue that way—so fast and direct and willing to reveal themselves."

"But it was because I was with you, right?"

Alexander meets my eyes. "Maybe."

I look at him.

"Declan, if I knew more I would tell you," he says. "But you have to understand that what's between us is new to me. I've never had to protect someone I have such intense feelings for. It scares me and I'm making up the rules as we go along. You're not even supposed to know we *exist*. Can you meet me halfway? Let me tell you more when it's sorted?"

I consider his request, brow furrowed.

"I love you," he says softly. "And I want to be with you. And, unfortunately, that puts a wrinkle in my plan. More than a wrinkle."

I search his eyes. "What wrinkle?"

"It's not important now. If it comes to that, I'll explain. And I'll need your help."

"I don't think you have a plan. I think you're making it all up so I won't worry."

He smiles. "You know that I do. I promise you, I have several."

"Then tell me what they are."

He takes a deep breath. "Let me try Plan A, which is talking, and if I get the information I want, and it's favorable, this could be done and dusted in no time. So why bother you with Plan B yet or myriad details that may never become necessary?"

"I'm worried about you being near Avestan," I say. "Even just to talk."

"The worry should be directed the other way 'round. If Avestan was smart he wouldn't come near me."

"Now you're just blustering."

He smiles. "Did I mention I love you?"

My lips form a begrudging smile and he bends to kiss me softly.

"I'll do whatever it takes to protect you," he says. "Always."

Chapter Five

"Liz is covered, I promise," says Alenna as we sit inside West End Coffee.

I nod. "Thanks." It's been two days since we found out Avestan is back in San Mar, and Alexander suggested we all meet to put my mind more at ease. "Did Avestan bring more dark guardians with him?" I ask.

"Unfortunately, yes," she answers. "Most lost interest and left to darker places while he was recovering, but now that he's back they've come back with him."

"Evil follows him," says Alexander.

I nod and swallow. "I know you said everyone is protected, but does that still include Charlie and his family?" The thought of anything ever happening to Charlie again twists my stomach in a knot. And even if Molly Bing is a Queen Bee jerk, she doesn't deserve Avestan.

"They're taken care of," answers Alexander. "And Edwin is covering Finn personally."

"Why can't all the guardians just protect everyone all the time?" I've asked this before and I know what they're going to say.

"There aren't enough of us," Alenna answers patiently. "We go where we're most needed. Mortals wouldn't gain the understanding they need to evolve if we stepped in every time things get messy. It's a delicate balance." She glances over at Alexander. "We could tell mortals everything we know but unless they experience it themselves, they tend not to listen. They have to make their own decisions."

I nod. Initially I had misgivings about how Alenna would feel about me since she and Alexander used to be together, but she welcomed me warmly from the start and she's always been kind. I have to practically avert my eyes to look at her, though. She's so beautiful—it's like staring up at the sun with her towering legs and all that blonde hair and porcelain skin—but I don't get the insecure pangs that I used to anymore. Well, I don't get them as *much* anyway ... I'm still a human woman for Pete's sake.

"So everyone's just double protected," I say, "and we should go about our day?" It feels strange to act normal now that Avestan's back, but it's not like I can round up everyone I love and insist we all cower inside.

"For now," Alexander says. "Avestan's been avoiding me. His message through Liz was meant to frighten you but he's not ready to engage yet. He may still be recovering or, more likely, he's enjoying keeping us off balance. It's down to him now to come out of hiding. Unless I can find him first."

Alexander's answer sends prickles of worry up my spine. I don't *want* Alexander to find him. Avestan obviously likes to feel as if he's the one with the upper hand and if Alexander surprises him his reaction will most likely be unpredictable and outsized.

"Can you at least tell me who all the guardians are that will be protecting us?" I know what they're going to say before I even ask the question, but I can't resist trying.

"It changes. And we can't reveal anyone," Alenna replies. "Mortals have to trust their instincts. But I'm sure you can work it out. You're good at reading people."

She's right in one sense—I *have* gotten better at protecting against negative energy and reading auras. When I shake someone's hand or touch their arm I can usually get a feeling about them. But I don't trust it enough to tell me definitively if someone's a guardian or a dark angel. They could just be a good person, or someone having an especially horrid day. Dark angels are adept at concealing themselves, and guardians take care not to be revealed either. I think Alenna's giving me way too much credit here.

"Alenna's right," Alexander says, "trust your instincts. After all, they're what led you to me." He takes my hand in his and his smile reaches his dark green eyes. For all of his frustrating withholding of information, he still makes my heart skip a beat when he looks at me that way.

Alenna stands up and clears her throat. "I think we have a good plan for now," she says. "Declan, are we still meeting later for aikido? See you there at six?"

I nod. "Finn's coming, too." A few months ago I bought a Groupon for an aikido class on a lark and made Finn come with me. The blurb online described it as redirecting energy so that you blend with an attack rather than meeting it head on, using your opponent's own energy against them. It sounded interesting, and Finn has anxiety underneath the surface like I do, so I thought it could help us both. We ended up liking it and Liz tried it, too, but she decided she'd rather stick to watching kung fu movies with us instead. Alenna stayed for a class once and now she goes regularly, too. Of course she could kick everyone's ass if she wanted to, including the instructors, but she says she likes the meditative aspect of it. I like that part, too, but mostly I like the fact that if I concentrate hard enough I swear I can react to what my opponent's going to do before they do it. In those moments I feel like Neo in *The Matrix* and I truly believe I'm a sprite with powers—someone who can kick ass and take names to protect myself—a feeling I'm particularly craving now because I feel pretty helpless with Avestan back and lurking in parts unknown.

Alexander searches my eyes after Alenna walks away. "Don't worry," he says as he plants a tender, reassuring kiss on my lips, "about anything."

"Because you have a plan," I say.

"Yes," he smiles, "because I have a plan. And also because you're strong. Stronger than you realize. And I have you covered."

"That's not what I'm worried about," I say.

"What is it then?" he asks.

I meet his green eyes as I expose the worry deep in my heart. "Who's covering *you*?"

Chapter Six

"This is simultaneously the least demanding and highest-paying job I've ever had," announces Justin, my co-worker at Fields and Morris, L.L.C.

I laugh. "It is pretty mindless." Burt Fields, my dad's old partner, hired a crew of college students (and prospective college students, in my case) to do a boatload of scanning and data entry at his firm. All we do, all day long, is retrieve legal documents from large file boxes and scan the pages one by one into the computer, add keywords for each file, and then start on the next piece of paper. When we're finished with a box we mark it with a giant "X" using a red Sharpie, add it to the "completed" side of the room and then we pull down a fresh file box from the stack of boxes lining the other wall. The rule is, if you start scanning the files in a box you must finish it entirely and at the end of the day we log how many file boxes we completed. Overtime is encouraged and I've taken advantage of it as often as possible. It's a short-term job, just for the summer (or until all file boxes are scanned and logged) but it pays well. The extra income is helping me sock enough away to cover the cost of my books and fees for school. I'm still working at Jack's, too, but that's mostly on weekends. And I fit in babysitting for Charlie Bing when I can. I'd do that for free, to be honest. I love that little guy.

"Did they have to put us in the room with no windows?" Justin says. "Janice and Chris have a window at least." Janice and Chris are two of our co-workers in another conference room down the hall. There's space for only two people and two computers and scanners in each room.

"It's like being in a casino," I say, "you can't tell whether it's day or night."

"They could take our phones and work us for 24-hours straight," Justin says, "and we'd never know the difference."

I chuckle. "Janice and Chris's window looks out over the air-conditioning unit in the parking lot," I say, "and it makes a lot of noise. I worked in there a few weeks ago."

"Yeah," he says, "I did, too. I'm just complaining to pass the time."

I smile. Justin is a nice guy. We've been assigned to the same conference room for several shifts and we've gotten to know each other well because there's simply nothing else to do other than talk to each other when you're stuck in a windowless conference room scanning documents mindlessly all day.

"Can I confess something?" he asks.

I look up from the page I'm scanning. "What?"

"I've been manipulating the work assignments for the last week so that you and I end up in the same room."

"Why?"

"Because Chris has bodily function issues and all Janice talks about is her cats."

I'm in the midst of taking a sip from my water bottle and I nearly spit it out as I laugh. "What bodily-function issues?"

"He devours five-pound burritos from the Spicy Monkey food truck across the street," Justin proclaims as if the explanation is more than enough. "Never get assigned to the windowless room with Chris," he adds. "Trust me."

I laugh. "How do you manipulate the work assignments?"

"I'm just nice to Nora, the receptionist," he says. "She's the one who makes the project sheets and I asked if she wouldn't mind assigning us together."

I nod.

"That okay with you?"

"Sure," I say with a shrug. "Janice is nice enough, but I've *been* assigned to the windowless conference room with Chris."

He laughs.

"Thanks for asking me, though," I add as we both pull out yet another legal document from our file boxes to feed into the scanners.

Alenna and I are on our way to get a juice smoothie after aikido class but Finn had to leave so he'd have enough time to shower before meeting up with Liz.

"Who's guarding Finn right now?" I ask as we watch him disappear on his bike around the corner.

"Don't worry," Alenna says with a touch of her hand on my forearm. "There's always someone nearby."

"And you haven't seen Avestan?"

"Alexander will find him," she says. "Try not to worry if you can. It will all work out in the end."

Her answer isn't exactly reassuring. I hate it when people say that. What does it even mean? What if it works out badly?

"So how are things with you and Alexander?" she asks as we walk past the shops downtown to Jamba Juice.

"Fine," I say with a vague nod. I'm leery about talking about Alexander with her and hurting her unnecessarily.

"Declan, Alexander is my friend ... and so are you now. I've never seen him light up the way he does when he's with you. I'm happy he's happy. I hope you know that."

I nod, smiling. "Thanks. We're doing great."

"You're breaking new ground, you know."

"What do you mean?"

"A guardian and a mortal. Or a sprite, I should say. Although I did hear something about a guardian falling to be with a mortal once before."

"Really? I thought they couldn't do that, because they'd start over?"

She shrugs. "It's probably just a story."

I nod, unsure what to make of her disclosure.

"If you don't mind my asking," she says, "how does that work between the two of you? When you, you know…"

"Huh?" I ask, startled out of my mind-wanderings.

"You know what I mean…" she says with a sly smile.

"Are you talking about *sex?*"

She laughs. "Just between us girls. I've been wondering … because with the difference in strength, how does that work? How can he let go with a mortal? I don't know a lot about sprites, so I guess I'm just curious … you can tell me to shut up at any time here if you want." She smiles apologetically.

I don't answer at first. If I was going to talk to anyone about this kind of thing it would be Liz, first and foremost. But I can't talk to Liz, or my mom, because they have no idea Alexander is a guardian. How would I explain to them that one of the reasons Alexander and I haven't had sex is because he's so strong he's afraid he might hurt me by mistake? Meanwhile, here stands Alenna, who, admittedly, I don't know all that well, but she's so nice and easy and open, and, when I think about it, she's really the only one I can talk to who knows the whole story. I mean, who else is there? Edwin? I almost laugh out loud at the thought of having a talk about angel sex with him. And that's why, as I circle over all of these thoughts in my mind, I find myself deciding to answer

Alenna with complete and utter candor. "Well I don't know much about sprites either," I say. "I'm still trying to figure out what it all means and what I can do. I don't have your strength—I know that much. But honestly, Alexander and I haven't crossed that bridge yet, so I couldn't answer your question even if I wanted to."

"You haven't?" The expression on her face is pure incredulity.

"He says he's worried about his strength," I explain. "And I don't know … I wasn't sure how ready I was either. But lately I've been wondering if there's something more to it than what he's saying. Do you know?"

She shakes her head slowly. "I have no earthly idea," she says. "Just between you and me that was never a problem before, if you know what I mean."

I know exactly what she means and despite her laugh and the way she nudges me jokingly I'm starting to hate her a little right now.

She sees the look on my face. "Oh, Declan, I'm sorry. I didn't mean anything by it. Sometimes I put my foot in it without thinking. The strength issue is real. That must be the reason. I'm sure otherwise he'd want to. I don't think it's because he's having second thoughts about being with a mortal." She puts her arm around my shoulders and gives me a quick hug for reassurance.

I nod, partially mollified at first, but her words: *"I don't think he's having second thoughts,"* hang in the air.

Maybe he doesn't want to?

My insecurities start to take hold but before they form roots my inner drill sergeant yells at me to stop being an idiot. Suddenly it all becomes clear: how foolish I've been, wondering and waiting and not saying anything. Alexander is open and honest … we talk about everything. All I need to do is ask him. I don't know why I haven't already.

Actually, that's a lie. I do know why.

For the exact reason Alenna just teased out.

I know Alexander loves me, but maybe he's having second thoughts about being with a mortal and everything that goes with that decision.

I'm not sure what his answer will be.

Chapter Seven

"I have an idea," my mom says as we get ready to walk to the beach. It's the anniversary of my dad's disappearance and we always go to the ocean to remember. My mom has always said it's not a day to be sad, it's a day to remember how lucky we were to have him in our lives as long as we did. And it's a chance to communicate and let him know we're doing okay.

"What?" I ask as I fill my backpack with two bottled waters and two towels to sit on.

"Instead of balloons I thought we could use some of the extra sky lanterns from your graduation," she says. "They were so beautiful. And we have a lot left over."

I smile. "Sorry about that. I didn't realize I was ordering them by the case."

"It was meant to be," she says with a smile, giving me a quick hug. "We can use them for years."

I hug her back. That's my mom, always looking on the bright side.

We're quiet as we walk to the ocean, lost in our own thoughts. When we get there, we take the stairs down the cliffs to the beach where I set down my backpack and lay out our towels. We both kick off our sandals and scrunch our feet in the sand. It's dusk and a few scattered groups of people have claimed fire rings to have bonfires on the beach later. My mom pulls the sky lanterns out of her large beach bag and hands me one. I can see there are already tears in her eyes and I give her a hug as mine well up, too.

"I'm sorry, honey," she says quietly. "I just miss him."

I nod and hug her tighter. "Me, too."

She kisses my cheek and pulls back, wiping a stray tear. "Let's do this," she says. "For your dad."

We walk toward the water with the sky lanterns in our hands and when we get to the edge, with the water lapping over our feet, my mom looks at me.

"You ready?" she asks.

I nod.

"Anything you want to say out loud?" she asks.

I shake my head. I'm too choked up to speak.

She nods and turns toward the sky. "I just want to say that we love you, Frank," she says softly. "And we miss you. And we know you're okay, wherever you are. And we are, too." Her voice cracks on the final sentence and she lights the thin layer of wax fuel for her lantern and then hands me the lighter so I can light mine. Then we both look at each other and raise our hands in the air and let them go.

As the round paper lanterns rise in the sky, beautifully lit from within, my mom and I hold hands and communicate the rest silently, from our hearts.

We watch as they get higher and higher, out over the ocean, until eventually the glowing messages to my dad disappear and flutter out in the night sky.

I hope you can hear us, dad.

We love you.

Chapter Eight

"Everything okay with you?" I ask Finn. We just finished a bike ride along the length of Seacliff Drive and now we've planted ourselves on a bench overlooking the ocean as we gulp from our water bottles. As I await his answer I peer around to see who might be watching us, good or bad, but everyone appears to be normal folk going about their day, not paying any attention to Finn and me.

"Why?" he replies.

"I don't know … you seem kind of down today."

"Down?"

"Depressed, I mean."

"No," he shakes his head. "It's not that. I looked it up."

"What do you mean you looked it up?"

"I thought I might be depressed so I looked it up online," he replies matter-of-factly. "My symptoms don't meet the criteria."

I meet his eyes. "Finn, just because your feelings don't match some list you found online doesn't mean that's the end of it. Something must have been bothering you enough that you looked up depression in the first place. What's wrong?"

"Nothing."

"Have you been thinking about that list you keep in your head? Of all the things to worry about?"

"It's not that."

"Are you sad about something?" I ask.

Finn is silent for a long moment. I can tell by the look on his face that he wants to form a precise answer. "I'm ... *conflicted*. I want to do something that I don't want to do."

My heart sinks as I wonder if he's trying to tell me that he wants to break up with Liz. "Is everything okay with Liz?" I ask tentatively.

"Yes," he says. "Why?"

"I don't know. I guess I was worried that you regretted not accepting a spot at Stanford."

"What are you talking about?" he asks.

"Isn't that one of the reasons you chose to go to UCSM instead of Stanford? Because of Liz?"

The expression on his face is utterly baffled. "What does Liz have to do with where I go to school?"

"Nothing," I say, relieved I'm wrong. "I guess I thought you might have wanted to stay close to her."

He stares at me, bewildered. I can almost hear the synapses firing in his brain trying to make sense of what I just said. "I chose UCSM because of the space sciences program," he says.

"Of course," I say. "Forget what I said. It's your life and your career at stake. I know Liz would choose the best school for her, too, regardless."

He nods and we both take a sip from our water bottles.

"Seventy-eight percent of romantic relationships that begin in high school don't last," he says.

I look over at him. "Is that what you're worried about?"

"No," he says. "It means that if it doesn't last it's probably not my fault. And it also means that twenty-two percent of them do."

I can't help but smile a little. "What is it then?"

Finn is silent for a long minute before he answers. "Can I ask you a favor?"

I turn to meet his eyes. Finn so rarely asks for anything I feel like he's giving me a gift simply by asking. Whatever he wants, I'm in. "Of course. Anything."

"Will you teach me how to drive?" he asks.

My eyes widen with surprise. "Yes," I say without hesitation as I absorb his request. In the past, Finn has been adamant that driving requires too much sensory input surging at him all at once and he wants nothing to do with it. "I thought you didn't want to drive, though?"

"My mom was sick last month and my dad wasn't home to drive her to the ER."

"Is she okay? Why didn't you call me?"

"It turned out to be nothing. But I'd been thinking about it even before that. I'm tired of relying on other people to drive me places that are too far to go on my bike. And I'm tired of the bus. It doesn't always go where I need to and it takes too long. Uber is okay but it's expensive for long drives. And truly driverless cars won't happen for years."

I nod. Of course Finn would have thought this through thoroughly. "I'm honored you asked me and of course I'd be happy to teach you."

"I'm not sure I'll be able to do it," he says.

His eyes meet mine and I can see that he's been fighting a war with himself over this. Finn avoids doing anything he thinks he might not be good at. It caused a lot of strife for him as a kid when he'd stomp off after losing a game or stop before the end of a game if he thought he might lose. I never, ever bring it up because he's embarrassed about it now, but I wish I could convince him he shouldn't be. We all did things as kids that we're embarrassed about now. Learning to accept losing was obviously excruciating for him but he somehow learned to deal with it. I suspect as he grew more confident in other areas it just didn't matter as much anymore. But he still prefers to stick to tasks in which he excels. And to be honest, who doesn't?

"You know what I think?" I say. "First of all, you don't really have to drive if you don't want to in today's world. There are plenty of other options and they keep getting better. Secondly, the last time you tried to drive you were fifteen and maybe you weren't ready yet. Our Driver's Ed teacher, Mr. Guilford, was a lunatic drill sergeant. I was in a state of terror the whole time we were in his car. Why do you think Molly Bing ran off the road into that fence?"

Finn laughs and I'm so happy to see his furrowed brow change to a smile. The "Barbie crash" or "B.C." as we came to refer to it, was a minor accident, no one got hurt, and Finn relished it gleefully because Molly had been needling him all day about what a lousy driver he was. Even so, I actually felt a little sorry for Malibu Barbie after we crashed. It could have just as easily been me that hit the gas and mowed down that fence in a panic while Mr. Guilford barked orders in our ears. Liz, to her never-ending regret, was assigned to a different Driver's Ed class that semester but she made us recount the story for her, in fine detail, many times.

"I think we should feel proud we managed to stay alive," I say. "Mr. Guilford scared the crap out of me."

Finn smiles. "He smelled like oranges and old comic books."

"He *did*," I say as I remember. "I can almost smell it now."

"I hate the smell of oranges," Finn says.

"Maybe because it reminds you of Mr. Guilford."

"No," he says, "I always hated it."

"I forgot about that," I say as the hard drive in my brain spins up a previously lost file. "I used to ask my mom to pack me grapes in elementary school because you wouldn't sit next to me when I peeled those Cutie oranges at lunch."

He looks over at me. "I hated those little oranges."

I laugh. "I like grapes better anyway. But getting back to your favor, you know who I really learned to drive from? Not Mr. Guilford."

"Your mom," says Finn, "I know."

"No. That's what my mom thinks, and she tried, but I was stressed out of my mind in the car with her. She used to correct me every second and it threw me into a panic. The person who really got me comfortable driving was Mrs. Denuzio."

"Your neighbor who was a hundred years old?" he asks.

"Ninety-five," I say. "I used to help her get groceries and one day she tossed me the keys and told me to drive. She was so laid back about it I was never stressed with her."

I think back to Mrs. Denuzio and her classic pale yellow Ford Mustang convertible. She used to say that everyone should know how to drive a stick shift and if I could drive her car I could drive anything. She instructed me on how to operate the clutch and gears exactly once and then let me figure it out for myself. Rarely did she say anything as we drove, or if she did, it'd be something like 'Now change lanes up here, doll, and look to your left because the rat bastards in this town don't know how to drive.' She always assumed I was in the right if someone honked at us. I loved that.

"Wasn't Mrs. Denuzio senile?" asks Finn.

"No," I say. "Well … maybe a little. But that's not the point."

"She can't teach me," says Finn. "She's dead."

"I *know* that," I say. "But I could be your Mrs. Denuzio."

"A senile teacher?"

"No," I say, shaking my head, "a teacher who's calm, with no stress. We just need to find somewhere quiet and peaceful where you can practice and we'll just take it little by little from there."

Finn nods. "I thought about asking Liz but I decided it's not a good idea."

I chuckle. He's right about that, if they want their relationship to survive. Liz can get 'overly excited' I guess is how I'd put it. "How are things going with you two?"

"That's another problem."

"Why?" My heart sinks.

"I bought her a gift last month."

"For what?"

"Our seven-month anniversary."

"Why seven?"

"I don't know. She kept mentioning it."

"Because seven's her favorite number?"

"Oh … maybe that's it …" he says. "I don't really know, except she kept saying our seven-month anniversary is coming up and I figured out eventually that she was trying to tell me something. She said six-month anniversaries are for chumps."

I laugh. "And that's a problem?"

"No. But I hid it at her house so if I forget the day of our anniversary it'll be there and I can still give her a present, on time."

"You *hid* it? At her house?"

He nods. "Then I worried she might find it, so I hid it again. And then I did that a few more times."

"And she found it?"

"No," he says. "I forgot where I hid it."

I can't help but laugh. "Seriously?"

Finn looks pained and I immediately wipe the smile off my face. *Oh Finn, only you could remember every word from an arcane scientific article you read three years ago and not remember where you hid your girlfriend's anniversary present.* "We'll find it, Finn," I reassure him with my hand on his shoulder. "Don't worry."

"Maybe I should get her something else. Just in case."

"Did you get her an actual present? Or a card with money in it?"

"A card is a present."

"You're right. I shouldn't have said that. So you got her a card?"

"She tried on a silver ring when we were at the artist's fair downtown and I bought it when she went to the bathroom," he says. "I remembered what you said about paying attention to things she likes."

Finn's earnest sweetness always gets me. He works so hard to do the right thing. "You're a good man, Finn," I say as I meet his eyes. "We'll go to her house next time she's at work and tear the place apart until we find it. Okay?"

"Okay. But we can't tear it apart."

"Figure of speech," I say with a smile.

"I know," he says as we stand up to get back on our bikes. "At least, I was pretty sure."

Chapter Nine

"Do you feel ready?" I ask Alexander.

"Ready for what?" he replies. He's driving me to my shift at Fields and Morris.

"Ready for you and me to … you know."

He smiles and looks over at me with a raised eyebrow. "I *know*?"

"C'mon, you know what I mean. Are you ready for us to sleep together?"

"We have slept together. Many times. I love waking up next to you. I even love the way you snore." He smiles and his green eyes crinkle so irresistibly that I almost don't want to smack him.

"I don't snore," I insist. On occasion we've spent the night together at his house or mine but I'm certain I would have known if I was snoring.

"It's cute," he says. "You're like a little koala bear … with a cold."

I look at him. "Well you're like a grizzly bear … with a fever."

"And here I was thinking you liked spooning with me," he says, feigning offense.

"I do," I admit. "You keep me warm."

"Well, you don't snore," he concedes, "but you do hog the bed linens. And I don't know how you do it, but you even manage to yank off the pillow slips sometimes. Are you doing aikido in your dreams?"

The smile I was holding back breaks through. "Well you hog the bed," I say. "And you're getting me off track. You know what I'm asking."

"I *do* know what you're asking. But this is important. No bland euphemisms. It's not sleeping together, it's something else."

I look at him. "Okay, are you ready to have sex with me? Is that what you want to hear?"

"It's not just sex," he says, shaking his head. "At least it won't be with us. It's more than that."

"What do you want then? I feel like you're holding back, for some reason that you haven't told me."

"I thought we agreed to wait."

"We did," I say. "But I don't want to wait anymore."

He meets my eyes and I can literally feel the electric undercurrent between us, filling the space in the car. He pulls over to the side of the road and shuts off the engine.

"What are you doing? We're going to do it now?"

He bursts out laughing. "On the side of the road? Are you off your nut?"

"Well, what are you pulling over for?"

"Do you think I'm a bloody animal? I'm pulling over because this is a conversation that requires my full attention." He shakes his head with a mixture of bewilderment and amusement and takes my hands, still laughing.

I can't help but laugh too. "Well?" I ask. "What do you think about what I said?"

"I think I'm not sure where this is coming from. What do you really want to know?"

I take a breath and meet his eyes. "Is your strength the only reason you've been holding back?"

He looks down for a moment. "It was at first … but I have that nearly sorted. I've been avoiding it for a different reason."

My heart is in my throat. "Because," I swallow, "you're not attracted to me anymore?"

"*What?* Declan … oh, babe, did you really think that?"

"I thought maybe you were having second thoughts," I say softly, "about being with a mortal."

He shakes his head. "I'm sorry I haven't put my side of it across. If anything I'm too attracted to you."

"Really?"

"If you only knew," he says, searching my eyes.

I swallow the lump in my throat. "I'm afraid that it won't be as good," I say quietly, "or as satisfying … with a mortal, or sprite, or whatever I am. Because you have to hold back. And on top of that, I'm not experienced."

He squeezes my hands. "That's what you're worried about? Think about how we feel when we're together. The way we feel when we kiss. It's going to be so good for us—better than we could ever imagine."

"You don't know that."

"I do," he says. "Sex isn't about gymnastics. It's about trust. And communication. Like this conversation we're having right now. It's about being vulnerable together and giving as well as receiving. And when you love each other, it takes it to a higher level."

"So why are you holding back then?"

"You're going to laugh," he says wryly.

"Why?"

"Because I have a plan."

"Are you kidding?"

"It's a plan I'm pretty sure you'll like," he adds with a smile.

"You always have a plan," I say. "For everything. But, you know, sometimes you have to *share* those plans ..."

"Or what?"

"Or people get suspicious," I say, looking up into his eyes.

"People?"

"Okay, me."

He smiles. "All you have to do is ask."

"I thought that's what I was doing, but you've got me going in circles."

He takes a deep breath. "Did you know that the English language has more words than any other?"

"What?"

"It means we can be precise because we have so many words to choose from to convey exact meaning. But it also means there are loads of words and terms for everything. And when we're talking about something as important as what we're talking about, I just want to get it right, so we both know how much it means."

I nod, still not quite understanding as he looks deep into my eyes.

"Making love. I want to *make love* to you, Declan. It may sound old-fashioned but out of all the messed-up ways people use to describe sex, it's the best I know. I want to connect with you and share that with you and make you feel intensely good and show you how much I love you. Does that make sense?"

I smile and my eyes well up. "Yes," I whisper.

"Is that what you want, too?"

The earnest look in his eyes goes straight to my heart and softens all my insecure, vulnerable edges. I nod and smile. "Yes."

He squeezes my hands in his and looks at me so lovingly my heart aches in my chest. "To be able to connect with you in that way," he says, "like our first kiss. That's why I've been holding back. I have a plan that I've been working on and as much as I've wanted to chuck it to the wind many, *many* times, including right here, right now, on the side of the road," he mimics tossing something out the car window and we both laugh. "I want to make it especially memorable. We only get one first time together and you know how I feel about a right time and place for things. We're going to remember this for eternity."

I smile.

"Can you hold on a little while longer?" he asks.

"I think I can control myself," I say dryly.

He laughs and kisses me. "I love you," he says with a smile.

"Me, too," I say. "So there's no other reason?"

He shakes his head. "The only thing between you and me and hot sex right now is my plan."

I laugh and push his arm. "Oh, so now it's hot sex? I thought it was 'making love?'"

"Now that you understand how much it means to me, you can talk about hot sex all you want. In fact, please do." His smile and the glint in his eyes make me laugh.

"The anticipation makes it sweeter," he adds.

"I remember." I think back to our first kiss and how it felt to finally have his lips on mine.

He smiles and gives me one last soft kiss. "Is that everything you wanted to talk about?"

I nod and smile in a happy daze until he restarts the car and I notice the clock on his dashboard. "Ah shoot, now I'm late for work."

Alexander glances over at me. "I think we can both agree that this conversation was well worth it."

We smile and chuckle as he pulls back onto the road.

"If your boss is cross," he adds, "let me know if you want me to come in and tell him it was my fault for ravaging you like an animal on the side of the road."

I push his arm and we both laugh. And for the rest of the drive, every time we glance over at each other, we smile and laugh again.

God, I love Alexander.

Chapter Ten

"I need some of whatever you're on," Justin says as we're busy scanning documents.

I look up from the file I was logging in. "What?"

"You look so happy," he says. "It can't just be that we got the room with the window today."

"No," I say airily as I pull another document from the file box in front of me.

"Then what is it?"

I shrug my shoulders and sigh. I can't seem to wipe the silly, swoony grin off my face after my conversation with Alexander earlier. "I just have a great boyfriend," I say finally, sounding like a lovesick fool, I'm sure.

"Did he propose or something?"

"No," I trill, "he's just sweet."

Justin shakes his head and smiles. "Girls," he mutters to himself as he feeds another document into the scanner. "So what do you want to talk about today?" he asks after a short stretch of silence. "Besides your sweet boyfriend."

"Very funny." I toss my empty water bottle at his head.

He holds up his hand and bats it away. "I'm just kidding. I'm sure he's a nice guy," he says. "I hope he deserves you," he adds after a beat.

I look up. "Awww," I say dramatically, "did you just say something nice about me? I better log this in the file." I pretend to type on my keyboard. "Day 19, Justin compliments Declan for first time."

He laughs. "I've complimented you plenty. I already told you I bribed Nora with chocolate just to get us assigned together."

"You never said you used chocolate, you just said you were nice to her."

He smiles. "I'm nice to her and I gave her chocolate, which is also nice."

"That's true," I say.

"Actually," he says, his voice trailing off, "maybe not. Remember when we were talking the other day about my philosophy class? I would, of course, always be nice to Nora—she's a nice lady—but I probably wouldn't have given her chocolate unless I wanted something."

Justin is a year ahead of me in school, also attending UCSM, and during the last shift we worked together we talked about the classes he took last year, one of which, his favorite, was Philosophy. "So you're saying your intent wasn't nice?"

"I don't know. Does the fact that I wanted something in return make it not nice or not pure?"

"Did you hold the chocolate hostage until she gave you what you wanted?"

"I didn't send a ransom note if that's what you're asking," he laughs. "I surprised her with her favorite chocolate muffins and then I asked if she wouldn't mind changing the project sheets, knowing she'd be more likely to want to help me."

I nod and tilt my head as I consider how to respond. "You took the time to find out that she liked chocolate muffins and then you requested something that was easy for her to do and harmless. That sounds like a prime example of how the birth of civilization and cooperation got started."

"You're right. It was smart," he says. "No more Chris and his Spicy Monkey burritos."

I laugh.

We both take a moment to type in some keywords to log a document and then we grab another paper from our file boxes. "Why was Philosophy your favorite class?" I ask.

"I liked the teacher, Professor Blakely, and I liked how the concepts made us think. He posed a lot of questions that were hard to answer."

"Like what?"

"Well, take utilitarianism, which is about ensuring the greatest good for the greatest number. It sounds good, but he'd give us these scenarios and it seemed like it would be easy to choose what to do but it wasn't."

"What scenarios?"

"Ethical dilemmas. Like this famous one called the Trolley Problem."

"What's that?"

"You're supposed to imagine you see a runaway trolley barreling down some railway tracks," he says "and up ahead, there are five workers unaware. You happen to be standing next to a switch that could divert the trolley to another track where only one man works alone. The question is, do you pull the switch and kill one person rather than five?"

"What do you think you'd do?"

"I'd pull the switch."

I think for a moment and decide to play devil's advocate. "I don't know … could you really pull a switch that would cause a man's death?"

"Yeah, but if you *don't* pull it five other guys are going to die."

"But if you don't do anything, it's an accident," I say. "Otherwise somebody dies on purpose."

He shakes his head. "People are going to die no matter what. You have the power to make it one person rather than five. I don't even think it's a choice, it's more like your duty to pull it."

"Your duty?"

"Yeah, if you're standing there and you can influence the outcome for the better, don't you have a moral obligation to do it?"

"Yeah, probably," I say. "It just feels wrong."

"Then you're really not going to like the next part," he says.

"What next part?"

"Everybody in our class said they'd pull the switch in the first scenario, but then our professor changed it up a little. Same deal, trolley's hurtling down the tracks toward five unsuspecting workers. Only this time there's no lever. Instead, you're on a footbridge overlooking the tracks and there's a very large man standing next to you. If you push the man onto the tracks into the path of the trolley to stop it, the five workers will be saved. Do you do it?"

"Oh my God, of course not," I say.

"Yeah, I know, everyone agreed … but Professor Blakely pointed out that from a strictly utilitarian perspective, the outcome is the same. You'd still be saving five people."

"Only now you're killing a man on purpose."

"Yeah, but that's why you hesitated before, because even just pulling the lever felt like you were killing someone on purpose. But most people are willing to pull the lever but not push the man."

"Well now the lever *is* a man. It's murder."

Justin nods. "The argument is that harm wasn't intended in the first scenario, it was only a side effect of pulling the lever. But in the second scenario, your *intent* is to cause the man's death."

"It's evil."

"Right, we talked about that: deliberately intending harm, even for good causes, is wrong."

"None of those scenarios are realistic," I say.

"Yeah, we said that in class, too. They're just academic exercises. But I was thinking about driverless cars. If a pilot in a plane is going to crash, steering to the least populated area is the right thing to do. But what about a car? Somebody has to code that software, right? If it's headed for a crash with five people and it can turn and hit only one, should it be programmed to do that? But what if it's going to hit a kid?"

During one of our shifts Justin told me that his mother and little sister died in a car accident when he was eleven. I think that's one of the reasons this discussion is obviously weighing on him. And one of the reasons he and I connect so well. We both experienced tragedy at a young age. "I don't know," I say. "The questions are hard."

Justin looks up from his train of thought. "Yeah, I don't know why I liked that class so much. The problems mostly just gave me a headache."

"Me, too," I say.

"How's it going in here?" asks Mr. Fields as he bursts through the door to our conference room, startling us both. I nearly jump out of my seat.

"Great," I say, once I recover. "We're making good progress." I gesture to the stack of finished boxes with large red x's lined up against the wall.

He nods, impressed. "Focused, just like your dad was. At this rate, you'll be out of a job before the end of the summer. Better slow down," he says jokingly.

I smile wistfully at the mention of my dad. "No worries, I think we'll be busy for a while." I peer over at the tall stacks of file boxes against the other wall still waiting to be scanned.

"Well," he says, "I came down because we had a catered lunch today for some clients and there's a bunch of sandwiches and drinks left over in the large conference room up on the second floor. Feel free to take a break and go grab some."

"Thanks," Justin and I say in unison.

"Can you let the other kids know?" he asks.

I smile. I assume by 'kids' he means Janice and Chris. "Sure."

He turns to walk out and we rise to follow him. We make a right outside the door to go find Janice and Chris and Mr. Fields goes left in the direction of the elevator.

"Declan," I hear him call out my name and I turn to see him pressing the button for the elevator. He waves me over and I tell Justin I'll be back in a second.

"Yes?" I say when I reach Mr. Fields.

"I've been meaning to ask, do you know if Frank happened to keep any files at home?"

His mention of my dad's name startles me. "Files? You mean stuff from when he worked here?" My face scrunches, thinking. "I haven't seen anything."

Mr. Fields waves his hand dismissively. "It's not important. I'm working on a case that relates to one he was working on a long time ago. If you happen to see anything related to the office, I'd appreciate it if you'd bring it in. Otherwise, don't worry about it. It was just a thought."

I walk back to join Justin. Why would Burt Fields want files from almost ten years ago? And why wouldn't they be in the Fields and Morris computer system anyway? Then again, what do I know? We're obviously being paid a large sum of money to digitize all these files for the lawsuit they're working on, and there's also some old files mixed in that they want stored electronically. Maybe a lot of legal documents are passed around in paper form. I forget about it as I enter the windowless conference room to join Justin in giving Janice and Chris a heads up about the sandwiches.

Chapter Eleven

"You sure you want to do this?" Alexander asks.

I nod. "I'm sick of waiting."

"You're certain? I think we should wait."

I shake my head. "Avestan's been back for two weeks now. Anything could happen any day. I don't want to wait any longer."

Alexander nods, obviously unconvinced. We're at our spot on top of the San Mar Mountains and it's a clear day with just a few soft, billowy clouds in the sky and a light breeze blowing over us. We stand up and walk over to the edge of the precipice and when I peek over I instinctively back up nervously at the steep drop off to the ground far below. My heart is pounding.

"I wish we wouldn't do this," he says.

"I know."

"There's no guarantee it will work."

I swallow. "Please. I just want to do it. I want to try."

"Okay," he says with a heavy sigh. "Face forward and look out to the ocean."

I do as he says, steeling my resolve. "I want you to—"

Before I can finish I feel his hands at my back pushing me over the edge and now I'm gasping and plunging to earth. All the preparation in the world hasn't readied me for this and my heart seizes in my chest as I realize I've made a dreadful, horrible, *what-the-hell-was-I-thinking* mistake. I summon every ounce of focus I can, trying to find my center and concentrate, but it's no match for the terror chasing me as I tumble and fall, gaining speed. 120 miles per hour is the terminal velocity of a human body, *isn't that what Finn once said?* It's funny what you remember when you're plummeting to your death. At 120 miles per hour I'll stop accelerating until I ... oh my God, *what was I thinking?* This will never work. I can't focus. I can't find my core. Do I even *have* a core? Why did I do this? Why did I—.

At barely an arm's length from the ground I'm embraced in a sweeping whoosh and transformed into light energy. I feel myself powering up to the sky until I'm atop the mountain again, becoming solid flesh bit by bit from the feet up. Alexander and I re-appear face to face, arms wrapped tightly around one another. Normally I want to kiss him after we fly together but this time the flight was too short and the memory of being scared is too strong and I honestly feel like crying ... or slapping him. I don't know which.

"Hey, it's okay, it's okay," he says, cradling my face in his hands. "Are you all right? I think you got your answer."

"Why did you wait so long?" I ask, still gasping for air.

"Declan," he says, meeting my eyes, "did you think for a moment I would ever let anything happen to you? Anything at all? You made me promise to wait ... we went over it again and again. And you made me promise to push you when you weren't expecting it. You said you had to be truly scared or you wouldn't know for sure. It killed me to do it."

I nod. I can see the anguish in his eyes and he's right. I pressured him over and over until he had no choice but to relent and do as I asked. I feel him flooding me with his energy and I take a deep breath, drinking it in. Alexander always feels so wholly, utterly good. I melt against him as the feeling takes hold.

"So you can't fly," he says softly, tucking the stray lock of hair that always falls over my eyes behind my ear. "It's okay."

I nod but inside I'm sorely disappointed. We've been trying to figure out my powers as a sprite. *Powers*—it feels funny to say that when I've been at the mercy of panic attacks and anxiety my whole life. To finally be in control and realize I actually have *powers* to call on is almost laughable. Only I can't call on them at will … not in any meaningful way. The only thing we've figured out so far is that I can read people, I have fast reflexes, and when I'm in a life or death situation (like, for instance, when a dark angel named Avestan is in the process of killing my boyfriend before my very eyes) I can somehow use my energy as a force. Otherwise it's little bits of light energy here and there that I can sometimes call on but nothing substantial. And, oh yeah, the foot warming thing when I'm surfing—nice, but not exactly a scary deterrent to dark angels. I was hoping I might also have the ability to fly, like Alexander, and I had this crazy idea that if I put myself in a life or death situation maybe I'd be able to tap into any latent powers instinctively. It feels stupid now, but the idea of waiting until a *true* life or death situation to find out what the heck I can or can't do is terrifying. However, in retrospect, telling Alexander to push me off a cliff unaware was pretty dumb … that's what fear of dark angels will do to you: turn you into an idiot.

The bottom line is I wasn't able to fly. Months of focusing and trying to harness my energy has yielded no new powers. But when I remember how my love for Alexander sparked his energy back to life after we escaped Nusquam, I know, somewhere within me, I do have power. But maybe it was a one-time-only-you-use-it-and-lose-it-like-a-bee-stinger kind of thing. In that case, it's still an ability I'm forever grateful for. Without it, Alexander wouldn't be here right now.

Alexander looks down into my eyes, still holding me in his arms. "I know you really wanted to try this, but I'm pretty sure the only way you're going to find out your powers is organically."

"Maybe you should have shared that little nugget of wisdom before I hurtled to my death a few minutes ago."

He laughs. "For the record, I did, several times, but you wanted to try it anyway and I've learned not to get in the way of Declan Jane's ideas."

"Very funny."

"It's true. You're fierce when something matters to you. I'm not surprised you knocked over Avestan when we were in Nusquam."

"But I can't do anything powerful on command."

"That's not true," he says as takes my hand and tugs me over to the picnic blanket we laid out on the ground earlier, so we can sit down. "Do you remember when you wrote D.J. loves A.R. with your light in mid-air? That was before you even knew you were a sprite. When your heart's involved, your power comes out."

I smile.

"That startled me speechless, by the way," he says with a laugh. "From the moment we met, you had me confused and mesmerized."

"Ditto."

Alexander smiles. "I brought some muffins," he says as he leans over and reaches into his backpack. He reaches around inside and then yanks the backpack closer and peers inside, unzipping pockets. "Argh," he says as he sets the backpack down, empty-handed, "I must have left them back in Woody."

"Woody?"

"My jeep.

"Your jeep has a name?"

"Yeah, she's called Woody," he says casually. "I always name my transportation."

"Really?"

"Yes. Why are you looking at me funny? Your car's called Archie."

"Woody? Because of the wood paneling?" He has a classic white Jeep Wagoneer with wood paneling.

He shrugs. "Seemed right."

"I guess I'm just surprised I didn't know that. I thought I knew everything about you by now."

"There's a lot you still don't know about me."

"I think I know you pretty well," I say with a measure of skepticism. "I know you're an angel … I know all your powers … you told me all your history—for most of your lives at least—and I found out, on my own, that you're very ticklish," I say as I reach my fingers along his side, "over here."

"Ah!" he bellows as he wrestles me down and straddles me, pinning my hands above my head.

"You know," I say, laughing, as he looks down into my eyes, breathing hard, "you've got a fatal flaw for a guardian angel. All anyone has to do is tickle you and you're done for."

He smiles. "Maybe I just let you *think* I'm ticklish so that I can get you in this position," he says with a wicked gleam in his eye. The air between us is electric as he holds my gaze and leans down closer, our lips only a breath away.

"But what if I wanted you to get me in this position all along," I say with a wry smile of my own.

Amusement lights up his eyes. "Clever girl," he says as he closes the distance between us and his lips meet mine—soft at first and then like he means it. I sigh as I melt into his kiss. He strokes my tongue with his, teasing and exploring, and tugs at my bottom lip as his hands still hold my arms above my head.

Then he pauses, his eyes dark and smoldering, and the energy between us vibrates with intensity.

"When is that plan of yours going to happen again?" I breathe softly.

"Soon," he murmurs as he presses his lips to mine again. "But not soon enough," he groans mid-kiss and we both laugh. We stay that way, laughing and kissing and enjoying our moment on the mountain, until eventually we sit up and look out over the trees to the wide blue swath of ocean in the distance. It's stunningly beautiful and I lean my head on his shoulder as we enjoy the view. After a while, I turn and kiss the edge of his jaw, breathing in deep the fresh soap and natural scent of him that I love.

"This would be a pretty perfect place," I say.

"For what?" he asks.

"Your plan."

He smiles, turning towards me. "You want me to chuck the plan?"

"Yes."

He laughs. "Me, too. But you're going to like it," he says confidently.

"I'm sure I will. But you're really stretching the bounds of anticipation."

"I take my anticipation very seriously," he says with a wicked smile and a glint in his eyes.

"I've noticed."

He laughs. "Right now, in this moment, I have another plan. A very simple one."

"What does it involve?"

"It involves kissing you. A lot."

He silences my laugh with his lips on mine and I forget about everything else in the world for as long as Alexander holds me in his arms.

Chapter Twelve

"Would you like some *Answers?* Are you feeling *Unfulfilled*? Would you like to know *Why Your Here* and how to reach your *Full Potential*?"

Everywhere I go I've been seeing these flyers all over town. The same words, over and over. Stuck on the windshield of my car, under the welcome mat at our house, stuck to the bulletin board at Starbucks. Everywhere I turn, the whole town is blanketed with them.

"*Find the Answers* you seek. The *Success* and *Riches* you deserve. Gain *Free Insights* into your personality. Come to our Fun Fair or visit us on Ocean Ave."

Other than the date and time for the fair, the only other information is the name at the bottom: *SoFT: The Society For Truth. We have the answers.*

Liz and I pull the flyers out of the baskets on the front of our bikes parked at a rack on Seacliff Drive before we put our backpacks into the baskets instead. We've been at the beach all morning, hanging out and body surfing. Now Liz has to leave for work at Jack's but I, amazingly, have the rest of the afternoon off until I babysit Charlie later tonight. Alexander's meeting me here so we can go to the movies.

"I've been seeing these everywhere," she says. "What the hell is SoFT?"

"No idea. But they obviously don't care about killing a zillion trees."

"I almost want to go to their Fun Fair," says Liz, "just to see what it is."

"You're nuts."

A. J. Messenger

"Actually," she says, "I'm fascinated with nuts—nuts who leave redonkulous paper flyers with glaring typos everywhere instead of harnessing the power of the interwebs."

I laugh.

"Hey, Alexander," Liz calls out with a nod, her focus shifting past me.

I turn my head to see Alexander walking up to join us. "Hi, Liz, how ya going?" he replies. He wraps his arms around me from behind and kisses my cheek. "What's this?" he asks, peering over my shoulder at the SoFT flyer in my hand.

"We keep finding these all over town," I reply. "I was just about to toss it."

I hand it to Alexander and he skims the contents before crushing it into a ball and pitching it into the nearby recycling bin.

"Guess that means you don't want to go to their Fun Fair with me," says Liz dryly.

Alexander shakes his head. "Rubbish."

"Wow," she says, eyeing Alexander sideways, "is it just me or do you seem more opinionated than your usual self? Maybe waking up every day in the wrong hemisphere is finally getting to you?"

Alexander smiles. "Nah, just looking out for you, love."

She smiles. "But I was going to get some 'free insights into my personality' from these people," she says jokingly, still waving the flyer in her hand.

"You're a larrikin," says Alexander. "There's your free insight."

Liz peers at him quizzically. "Do you realize that half the time I have no idea what you're talking about? What's a larrikin?"

Alexander laughs. "Someone who would tell Molly Bing to get over herself when she tried to push you off her lunch table in primary school ... a cheeky, good-hearted person."

"It was middle school," Liz says, forming a slow smile. "You're saying I do the right thing, in other words."

"You don't care what others think," he says. "You break the rules if you have to and you don't waver. You know yourself."

Liz's eyes flash with pride and approval. "Hmm," she says as she gets onto her bike. "I really hate to end this fun chat about how great I am but I'll be late for work. Declan, do you have a Jack's T-shirt? I forgot mine."

I laugh. "Jack bet me five bucks you'd forget today. Don't tell him I told you but I think there are some extras in the cabinet in his office."

"Ha!" she says, "See? That's the solution. I don't see why he gets so bent out of shape about Hula Burger t-shirts. See you guys," she says with a smile as she maneuvers her bike onto the path and takes off.

"Bye, Liz," Alexander and I call out in unison.

"What was that all about?" I ask Alexander after she's gone.

"What? You mean about the flyer? I shouldn't have said anything." He pauses a moment. "I think I'm just frustrated I haven't been able to find Avestan and I'm tired of—" He stops himself.

"Of what?" I ask.

"I don't know, all of it. I'm tired of the dark guardians ... and I'm tired of these groups that tell vulnerable people they have all the answers and end up taking all their time and money, promising them whatever they're looking for."

"Do you know this group?"

He takes a deep breath. "There are no shortcuts. To anything. Just work hard, follow the golden rule, and listen to your better angels when you're not sure. We're all connected," he says with intensity, "we're all in this together. That's all anyone needs to know."

I look up at him. "Maybe you should put that on a t-shirt."

He smiles, breaking out of whatever mood he was in. "Maybe I should," he says. "Do you think Liz would wear it?"

I laugh and push his arm and he gives me a kiss.

I arrive at the Bing's house and see Molly's BMW in the driveway. Ugh. *Why is she always here?* Before I can even ring the doorbell the front door opens and Molly is standing there. "You're here, finally," she says with bored irritation.

My eyes flick to my watch and back up at her. "It's 7:55. Your mom told me to get here at eight," I say.

"Whatever," she says. "She left early. I've been watching the brat since five. I gave him dinner. He's watching TV." She turns away and walks upstairs.

I walk into the family room and spot Charlie with Batman underwear on his head along with a Viking helmet and a foam sword in one hand and a vanilla milkshake from McDonald's in the other. He's standing in a half empty box of pepperoni pizza on the floor and I see what I can only describe as a ginormously-sized Slurpee cup with remnants of its previous bright cherry color contents on the end table. He turns and sees me and yells out, "Declan!" with a big smile on his face and runs over. Then he stops himself short of hugging me, remembering he's in disguise. He stares at me, sticking out the sword in front of him. "Have you seen that silly boy, Charlie?" he asks.

I can't help but laugh. I crouch down to his level and shake my head innocently. "No, I haven't seen Charlie. But I hope to. I'm looking for him. Who are you?"

He starts to answer and then he stops and gets a sick look on his face. "Declan?" he says quietly, sounding worried.

"Yes?" I say with concern. "What's wrong, honey?"

He gets an uncomfortable look on his face. "I think I have to go number three."

"Number *three?* What's numbe—"

He drops the milkshake and heaves forward, vomiting on me with a projectile force I wouldn't have thought possible for a five-year-old.

Thanks, Molly.

Chapter Thirteen

I awake early the next morning from a fitful night plagued at first by memories of cleaning up Charlie and me, (and helping the poor kid feel better after several more bouts of throwing up) and then, when I finally managed to fall asleep, by horrid nightmares of Avestan. He was chasing me and everywhere he went people would fall in line behind him, joining him. Finn and Liz, and even my mom, were following him as he made his way toward me, relentless and vile. The chase replayed several times, and at the end, when he had me cornered, Avestan would outstretch his hand and I'd accept it. Every time.

I drag myself out of bed, exhausted, and tug on my running clothes. Then I quickly go to the bathroom, brush my teeth, and gather my hair into a long ponytail with the elastic band I keep on my wrist. I stare into the mirror for a minute, blue eyes looking bleary, and say the words I always repeat to myself on mornings like this. "You want to go for a run. You don't want to go back to bed. You'll thank me later." My inner drill sergeant has a much more forceful way of putting it, but I don't wake her today—I'm way too tired.

As I walk back into my room to put on my running shoes, I hear my phone chime on my nightstand. I pick it up and see a text from Alexander.

Already at the beach.
I'll meet you here.

Lately he's been running with me in the mornings, I guess he left early. I shrug and tap in a reply.

K see you soon.

I planned to take it slow but once I'm out the door I push myself, hard. I don't know if I'm running toward Alexander or running away from the images of Avestan in my nightmares last night, but running to my limit forces me to focus only on the moment. My toes spring off the pavement over and over as my ponytail swishes rhythmically at the back of my head. It's a cool morning, overcast, and the waves are pounding the sand with ferocious savagery as I arrive and peer out over the beach. I spot Alexander near the water's edge and I wave to him before I make my way down the cliffs. When I reach the bottom, I take off my shoes and socks and scrunch my toes in the cool, rough sand the way I love. Alexander sees me but doesn't wave. He just stands there, waiting for me by the water. It's odd and I can't shake a feeling of foreboding as I make my way closer.

When I reach him I see that he's dripping wet. My eyes trail over his sculpted chest and abs to his board shorts hanging low on his hips and I notice an angry-looking abrasion on his left side. When I meet his eyes again I see that he looks tired. Exhausted even. Like me.

"Have you been swimming?" I ask.

He nods.

"How long have you been here?"

"A while."

"What happened?" I ask, gesturing to his side with concern.

He looks down at the abrasion. "Must have got tossed in a wave."

"Aren't you going to heal it?"

He shakes his head. "Later."

"Alexander, what's going on?"

A long stretch of silence hangs in the air between us and I feel myself becoming faint when he still doesn't answer. *Why is he being so distant?*

Finally, he looks at me and the words that he speaks are so unexpected, so unthinkable, that they don't register at first.

"Declan, I'm sorry, but we can't be together. I have to leave."

My heart falls through my center and I'm having trouble feeling the bottoms of my legs. "*What?*" I try to speak but the word emerges as a rush of air. I can't breathe.

"It's the only way," he says with grim finality.

I don't answer. I *can't* answer.

"I'm sorry, Declan, but I have to."

"Why?" I whisper.

"Leaving was always the answer. I didn't want to face it."

I watch those beautiful lips that can turn so easily into an irresistible smile and I can't connect that image with the ugly, unimaginable words they're forming now. "What about the plan?"

"It didn't work. Now I see that this is the only way."

"You talked to Avestan?" I ask.

He nods. "I found him last night."

"Did you get the information you needed?"

He turns and looks out over the ocean, silently. "It wasn't what I expected," he says finally. He meets my eyes. "So I have to leave. I'm sorry."

"You're *sorry?*"

"It's the only way," he says, his mouth pressed in a firm line. "I'm sorry."

"This can't be happening. I won't accept it. For how long?"

"I'm sorry, Declan, I-"

"If you apologize one more time I'm going to scream."

I search his eyes and I can see his pain is real but I remind myself that he's the one making this choice. He's the one tearing us apart.

"I came up with excuses for waiting," he says, "because I wanted more time with you. I always want more time with you …"

He holds my gaze and his image shifts out of focus as my eyes become glassy. I squint tight, twice, trying to shut out what's happening.

"I was fooling myself that it could be any other way," he continues. "If I was a true guardian to you I would have left San Mar before Avestan came back. I'm sorry, I—"

"Stop!" I shout, putting my hands over my ears to close out the madness. "Stop," I say again, almost a whisper this time. "Please. Just. *Stop.*"

We stare into each other's pain-soaked eyes for long minutes as the sound of the waves breaking on shore beside us fills the air.

Eventually Alexander turns and stares out to sea. "Did I ever tell you he was called Devin?" he says as he breaks the silence. "When he was my brother, in our last mortal life …"

I don't answer. Picturing Avestan as a regular person named Devin—and a brother to Alexander—is impossible to reconcile with the evil he emanates now.

"He was tough," Alexander continues. "When we played together we'd both get knocked about but he never wanted to stop … not until he won. I could *feel* how desperately he wanted to be the bigger one. The stronger one."

I don't reply as he continues to stare out over the ocean. "We were good mates," he says quietly. "I would have given my life for him. But when he started listening to the wrong voices I didn't see it … I *missed* it."

I stare at the firm line of Alexander's profile as the icy surf laps at our feet. Something about his expression takes me out of my anger for a moment. "You miss him," I say quietly.

He doesn't say anything as he stares out to sea.

After several minutes I break the silence. "Can I ask you something?"

He looks at me and nods.

"When we left Nusquam you bent down and whispered something in Avestan's ear when he was lying on the ground. Did I imagine that?"

"No."

"Is it private, what you said?" I ask.

He releases a heavy sigh in every sense of the word. "I told him what you just said to me: I miss my little brother." He turns and meets my eyes. "But Devin no longer exists. All the good bits and pieces were crushed a long time ago … and now I understand why."

"What do you mean?"

"He told me who his Maker is," Alexander says flatly.

"His what?"

"His Maker. The dark angel who turned him. All dark guardians have one."

Something about this news has my stomach churning in a knot.

"Why did you want to know who his Maker is?"

"Because if you can destroy the Maker, you destroy the whole line."

I remain silent as I absorb this information.

"Dark angels are forbidden to reveal their Makers but he played into my hands and couldn't resist telling me," he continues.

"Why?"

"Because of who it is," he says. Something in his tone knots my stomach again.

"Who is it?"

He shakes his head. "Someone who can't be destroyed." His voice is flat and his words radiate finality. I decide not to probe any further for now.

We're silent as another wave crashes and I search his eyes. "That's why you have to leave?"

"Avestan wants his revenge."

"On both of us," I say.

Alexander shakes his head. "No. On me. He needs to prove he's more powerful than me. He wants to win. If I leave, it will draw him away … and you'll be safe."

"But you'd have to stay away forever."

He meets my eyes. "That's the wrinkle."

I feel lightheaded as I realize what he's saying. "No," I say. "No, no, no … I won't let you! How could you say that? There has to be another way."

He takes my hands. "Declan, I love you," he says fiercely. "Avestan can see it when we're together. He'll destroy everything I love. So I have to change that perception, by leaving."

"Perception? So this is pretend?" My relief is nearly matched by the rawness I feel for him letting my emotions whipsaw so sharply. "But he'll suspect."

"The one thing I know is I can't defeat him here, where I'm worried about him doing you harm again. I have to draw him away so it's a clean fight … between me and him … alone."

"What if he doesn't follow you?

"When someone wants something bad enough they can't resist. He wants to defeat me. He can't do that if I'm not here. Plus, I'll go to a corner of the world where the balance of energy has tipped," Alexander says. "Evil draws evil. And I can do some good in places where guardians are fighting to restore the balance."

His plan is running through my mind and all I can think is that there has to be another way. "He *killed* you, Alexander. You were lifeless in my arms," my voice turns hoarse and tears spring to my eyes at the memory of holding him on the beach after we left Nusquam. "What if you can't defeat him? I won't let you do this."

"I'm stronger, Declan. I just have to take the fight away from here. Good wins out."

"You know that's not always true," I cry. "There has to be another way."

"It's the only way to end this."

"What if you don't win? And I'm not there to bring you back?"

"If it comes to that," he says, looking into my eyes, "I'll make sure he dies with me."

The tone of Alexander's voice and the expression on his face makes my legs nearly buckle beneath me.

I can tell he won't be dissuaded.

Chapter Fourteen

"Dies with you?" I ask, trying to keep my voice steady. "What are you saying?"

"Two guardians can merge and transform," Alexander replies. "Avestan wouldn't be able to hurt you after I'm gone."

"Do you think I care what happens to me if you're gone? What do you mean you'd merge and transform? Into what?"

"Our energy would continue, but not as we are now. He'd be gone. But I would, too."

"How is that different from when he tried to kill you before?"

"Before, I would have started over, in some capacity. When you merge, you're gone. You don't come back."

"Can a dark guardian do that to you?"

"They could," he says, "but they don't. They don't like to sacrifice themselves. We do it to them. As a last resort."

"So all the guardians could rid the world of dark guardians that way?"

He shakes his head. "Wherever there's light, there will always be shadow, too. And there has to be a connection between the two guardians who merge—in strength and energy and intent. The dark guardians resist ... and if it doesn't work ..." He shakes his head again. "I can't explain it all. I'm sorry."

"You'd be gone forever if you did this?"

"In this form. But so would Avestan. It's the best outcome. If it comes to that."

"Best for whom?"

"It would only be a last resort."

"You can't do this," I cry, my chest tight with emotion. "How could you even consider sacrificing yourself?"

"I would do anything to look after you and protect you. But I promise you I'll fight like hell so it doesn't come to that. It's selfish, but I don't want to leave forever. I don't want to be apart from you."

"How is that selfish?" I take his hands and meet his eyes, pleading with him to understand what I'm saying. "Alexander, please tell me you won't ever destroy Avestan in that way."

He holds my gaze as the wind whips my hair but he doesn't answer.

"Why can't we just stay as we are now?" I ask.

"Looking over our shoulders? Constantly vigilant with me worried about you and your family and friends? Avestan won't ever give up. He's back now and this has to end. I have to end it."

"How long will you go for?"

"As long as it takes for Avestan to follow me and for me to defeat him. Edwin and Alenna and the other guardians will protect you while I'm gone but Avestan is the greatest threat. Once he's gone you'll be safe. It's personal with him."

"When were you planning on leaving?" I ask quietly.

"Straight away. I want you out of danger."

"What about our plan?" I ask.

"This is the plan."

"No, I mean *our* plan."

The expression in his eyes shifts as he understands. "I didn't think you'd want to … now that you know I'm leaving."

I meet his eyes. "Alexander, I don't want you to go," I say, tears escaping. "And I'm angry with you for telling me like this." I stare into his eyes, my heart breaking. "But if you have to, I want us to connect in that way before you leave … because I'm so afraid you won't come back." I choke back a sob on the last few words and my chest heaves as the cavalcade of sobs finally erupts.

He wraps his arms around me. "Oh babe, I'll be back," he says, stroking my hair as my head lies against his heart and I add my tears to the salty ocean remnants on his warm, hard chest. "I promise that no matter what happens somehow I'll find a way to come back."

He holds me close and I surrender into his tranquil energy and the aura of soothing heat emanating from his body. Gradually I feel the white light in my core awakening as our energies meld into one. My breathing slows, and the tears fade, and I pull back and look up into his eyes. "Tell me your plan. For us."

"And spoil it?"

"If you don't tell me, I worry I won't ever know."

He touches my cheek. "You really want this?"

"Yes," I say softly, diving into the deep pools of his eyes.

"Let's move up the timeline then. I can put off leaving for one more day. I think we've waited long enough."

Chapter Fifteen

Alexander has been texting me all day since we left the beach this morning. Little messages here and there. Some are instructions for tonight. Others are sweet notes about how he's been thinking about me and how much he's looking forward to tonight. Our latest back and forth round has involved some NSFW descriptions of where he wants to kiss me first and how it will progress from there. By the time my shift at Fields and Morris is nearly over at ten to three, I can barely concentrate.

"I'm leaving early today," I say to Justin as I add the file box I just finished to the stack on the "completed" wall.

"No kidding," Justin says, "I think you left a few hours ago."

"What do you mean?"

"All that giggling and texting," he says. "Did you actually scan anything today?"

I smile. "Very funny. I did four boxes."

"Hot date with the sweet boyfriend?" he asks.

I blush. "Yes. I'm going home early to get ready."

"Lucky guy," he says as he picks up another set of documents and feeds them into the scanner.

Justin and I spend most of our time joking and ribbing each other but every once in a while he forgets the sarcasm and throws down a compliment with sincerity and it catches me off guard. He's a cute guy—blonde hair, blue eyes, very fit, with that whole hot-surfer thing going on. He's had three different girls pick him up from work in only the last four weeks. If he wasn't such a player and I wasn't head over heels in love with

Alexander, I might take a second look at him. As it is, he's a good friend. He's funny and nice and he helps make the time fly by.

"Do you ever wonder how they can afford to pay us all so much to do this job?" Justin asks as I'm logging in some final notes on the files I completed.

I shrug. "The firm's doing very well," I say. "When my dad used to work here they had a few tough years, though. I remember my dad offered to go without a salary for a whole year, to help keep the firm afloat. He and Mr. Fields were friends and my dad did all he could so the firm wouldn't go under."

"What happened?" Justin asks.

"I don't know. I think Mr. Fields lost a big lawsuit he was counting on or made some bad investments or something like that."

"How did they turn it around?"

"I'm not sure," I shrug. "I was only like ten when it all happened. Mr. Fields managed something, I think, or maybe it was just the economy picking up."

"Well, he's definitely doing well now," Justin says. "Did you see that Rolex he wears? And that Tesla in the parking lot? I heard Nora say he just got divorced for the third time and he pays more alimony in a month than she makes all year."

I glance over at him as I type. "My mom once said he had a wandering eye, so maybe that's what happened with all of his marriages." I think back to when I was younger and how jealous I was sometimes of the Fields kids and all the toys they had and the trips they went on. Their life seemed so golden—especially after my dad died. But now, looking back, I realize maybe it wasn't so rosy for them after all. My mom, dad, and I were always happy together, at least, even without a lot of fancy stuff.

"I don't know much about his life now," I continue. "He doesn't come to our house much anymore .... I used to be close to his kids, Jessica and Brian, but then they started going to private school and I didn't see them as much. They're a few years older than me."

Justin nods.

Talking about my dad has made me a little sad, and reflective, and I remain quiet as Justin goes back to his scanning. I finish the file I'm working on, power down my computer, and organize my workspace. When everything is in order, I pick up my purse, anxious to leave.

"Have fun tonight," Justin says as I stand up and push in my chair.

"Thanks," I say as I reach the door, "see you Monday."

I glide down the hallway to the side exit door and push it to swing out in the parking lot. The light breeze that greets my face in the late afternoon sun feels refreshing after being cooped up in a stuffy conference room all day, even if we did get the room with the window today. I force myself to smile wide and remember how practically giddy I am at the thought of seeing Alexander in just a few hours and finding out what he has planned. Somehow I've managed to push out of my mind what happens afterwards, when he leaves tomorrow.

"There she is," a hauntingly familiar voice says to my right as I stride away from the building.

I stop, frozen, as thick black fear washes over me. "Avestan." His name emerges as an unbidden whisper from my throat. I turn to see him standing, dark and tall, all in black, smiling with porcelain white teeth.

"You remembered," he trills darkly. His voice spills out like ink, coating me slowly until it forms a languid, growing stain on the pavement at my feet.

I look in every direction, chest tight and heart pounding, and spot only one lone man getting into his car in the far corner of the parking lot.

"There's no one here to help you," Avestan says, "but I suppose you could always use your sprite powers."

He spits out the words with acute derision and I turn in surprise to meet his mocking, invading eyes.

"Oh yes … I know all about what you are," he says.

"What do you want?" I ask, steadying my voice as much as I can.

"I think you know," he says slowly and as he looks at me with his ink black eyes I feel an icy stab that pierces my bones.

"I won't go with you," I say firmly, turning to walk away. "Anywhere." I feel darkness descending over me and I struggle to fend it off by imagining the white ball of light in my core blazing bright and growing stronger.

"Even just to talk? You may want to reconsider that stance," he says with measured smugness. "Or has Alexander already revealed to you the connection you and I share?"

I stop and my head turns involuntarily.

"That's a surprise, is it? That you and I have something in common?"

"You're lying."

Avestan sighs with dramatic boredom. "Is it just me, Declan, or do you also find it interesting that the 'good' guardians are always the one's withholding information, while the supposedly 'bad' guardians, like me, are the ones attempting to give you the truth? It's very tedious having to explain this to you over and over."

"I don't believe you."

"Consider this: do you believe Alexander would have told you he was a guardian if I hadn't forced his hand? And yet here I am trying to give you the truth—again—and, once again, you doubt me."

"You want to destroy me."

"You and your *sprite* power?" he says mockingly.

"I think you're afraid of me," I say, staring deep into the black pools of his eyes.

Avestan laughs. "Afraid? You're an *aberration*, Declan. I don't know what fantasies you've imagined in your mind about sprites, but I could strike you down, right here, right now—"

I hear the click of the door open behind us and relief ripples through me so thoroughly I nearly crumple to the ground. It's Justin. "Everything okay out here?" he asks as his eyes drift over Avestan suspiciously. I weigh engaging Justin in conversation but the last thing I want is to put him in any danger. "Yes," I say as steadily as I can. Then I add, "It's okay, Justin, you can go back inside."

Justin looks over at Avestan, glances back at me, and then looks at him again. For a long moment, the two of them stare at one another while my heart ceases to beat. *How can I get him to go back inside so he won't get hurt?*

Finally, Avestan breaks the silence. "I was just leaving. I look forward to seeing you and Alexander again," he says to me with a nod. "It's going to be an enormous pleasure." He turns on his heel and walks away and as the heavy thump of his boots on the pavement sounds off the distance between us, I struggle to keep my knees from shaking.

Justin places his hand on my shoulder. "You okay?" he asks.

I nod.

He looks at me. "I take it that wasn't your sweet boyfriend."

The absurdity of his comment hits me right in the soft underbelly of the brave façade I've been laboring to uphold.

I choke out a laugh and then, slowly, tears form. "No," I say, "far from it."

Chapter Sixteen

"So who is he?" asks Justin after Avestan has left. He has his hand on my back to comfort me.

I meet his eyes. "Why did you come outside?" I ask.

"I saw you talking to him through the window. At first I thought he must be your boyfriend but something about it didn't feel right."

I nod.

"Are you gonna tell me who he is?"

I shake my head. "He's just a guy," I say as I wipe away a tear that spilled over. "I wasn't expecting to see him. It threw me."

Justin is silent and I can tell from his expression he doesn't believe me.

"He's not a good guy," I add.

"No shit," he says. "I could feel whatever was going on between the two of you through the walls. It interrupted my scanning, and you know how much I enjoy that and hate to stop."

I look up at him and can't help but let out a laugh.

"There she is," he says with a smile. "My scanning partner. Do you want to come back inside and sit down for a while?"

"No," I say, looking around to make sure Avestan is still gone. "I just want to go home."

He meets my eyes for a long beat and I can tell he wants to say something more but eventually he just nods. "If that's what you want, I'll walk you to your car."

I drive home in a daze and when I get inside I see a note from my mom on the table reminding me that she's in Big Sur for the weekend with her old college friends Kate and Jonae. I walk up to my room and close the door before I pull out my phone to call Alexander. A wave of fear hits me again and I squint to hold back tears as I press his number through unfocused eyes. He picks up on the first ring.

"I can't wait to see you," he says with a smile in his voice when he answers.

"Avestan threatened me," I say, my voice wobbly. "And I—"

The tenor of his voice changes immediately. "Are you okay?" he demands. "Are you safe?"

"Yes, he confronted me in the parking lot at work but I'm home now and—"

"Stay inside," he orders. "I'm sending Alenna over and I'll be there straight after." I can feel his fury through the phone and I'm terrified about what he might do.

"Alexander, please don't—" Before I can finish my sentence I realize he already disconnected.

When Alenna arrives thirty minutes later she greets me with a hug and we sit down at the table in the kitchen and I tell her what happened.

"I feel responsible," she says. "I was supposed to be watching you. I don't think he would have approached you if I was nearby."

"I left work early," I say. "It wasn't your fault. I usually leave at five but I was going to meet Alexander."

She nods. "He mentioned something." She reaches across the table and places her hand over mine. "Can I make you some tea? Get you a glass of water? Something to eat?"

I shake my head. My stomach is too tied up in knots. "What do you think Alexander will do?" I ask.

She takes a deep breath. "I don't know. It wouldn't be smart to go after him … today especially."

I look up. "What do you mean, today especially?"

She shakes her head. "I shouldn't have said anything. It was supposed to be a surprise I think."

"What are you talking about?"

"Alexander was busy all day today, getting ready for whatever you two have planned tonight."

"And?"

"And …" she meets my eyes and I can see she's reluctant to go on, "he's been traveling all day … by light energy."

The implication hovers in the space between us. "So he's weakened? … Is that what you're saying?" I form the words as a question but it's rhetorical. I already know the answer.

She nods, silently.

My chest caves with the heartache of knowing that being weak won't stop Alexander. I stand up, reflexively, panicked, positioned to react but not knowing what to do. "We have to stop him," I say. "Avestan will kill him." My eyes plead with Alenna. "You have to go and help him. You and Edwin and every other guardian. You have to go, now, and help him."

She shakes her head. "Declan, I don't know where he is," she says. "And even if I did, it wouldn't matter. The malignancy between them can only be settled one on one. It has long roots, and it's personal."

I shake my head. "I don't care, you have to find him, you can't let him—"

I'm interrupted by the sound of a knock, or more of a thump. Something heavy hitting the front door.

Alenna and I look at each other and then I run for the door. Alenna quickly maneuvers in front of me and sticks her arm out protectively to keep me from going first. "We don't know what it is," she says.

She looks through the peephole and turns toward me with a cautious shrug. "There's no one there," she says.

Then she opens the door and my heart freefalls to the ground.

Atop my mother's cheerful welcome mat, Alexander is lying, covered in blood.

And he's not moving.

Chapter Seventeen

Alexander's limbs are bent perversely and I cease breathing, staring in horror at the sight before me. Alenna and I rush forward and I kneel down beside him and caress his bruised, misshapen cheek. His eyes are closed and he's on his side, crumpled awkwardly.

"Alexander?" I cry. "Alexander?"

He doesn't answer.

"Alexander," I cry again, "it's Declan." I feel for a pulse and look up at Alenna only to see tears in her eyes that match mine. "Please, Alexander," I plead, touching his cheek again. "Answer me. It's Declan, I'm here." I bend my head in desperation to kiss his swollen lips and that's when I hear a low moan.

I turn to look at Alenna. I can tell she heard it, too. "He's alive," I say and the relief that washes over me resurrects my faded heartbeat and allows me to breathe again.

"Let's get him inside," Alenna says hurriedly.

We carry him inside and as we position him on the couch he emits a painful groan. "Declan?" he moans. His eyes squint and then open slowly, blinking against the light.

"Alexander," I say with emotion, caressing his cheek as I kneel beside the couch. "What happened?"

"I told Avestan …" he says with obvious painful effort, "… to leave you alone."

"Why? Why did you do that?" I say with desperation. "You were weak. And now you're hurt!"

He peers down, surveying his swollen body and obviously broken bones. "You should see the other guy," he says through another groan.

I gaze into his eyes and I want to shake him for so foolishly putting himself in danger but I see that familiar glint has returned and, more than any other emotion flooding through me in this moment, I feel immense relief. "Why haven't you healed yourself?" I ask.

He looks down again to inspect the damage. "This is going to take a while," he says dryly.

I shake my head. "I thought you were dead," I say with emotion, "and now you're making jokes?"

He smiles and immediately winces with pain. "What better way to show you I'm okay?"

I look over at Alenna. She's standing at the end of the couch looking surprised and relieved. "Can you heal him?" I ask.

She shakes her head. "We have to heal ourselves."

I turn back to Alexander and he reaches up with noticeably broken arms and hands and guides me to him for a kiss.

"What are you doing?" I say with horror. "I can't kiss you when your elbows are pointed in the wrong direction."

He chuckles and instantly groans. "The key is to be gentle."

I smile and relent, bending to kiss his cut, swollen lips. Our kiss is soft at first, barely touching, and then he pulls me closer, bringing my lips against his and he kisses me with an ardor I wasn't prepared for—and to be honest am a little self-conscious about with Alenna in the room. But as the kiss goes on, I return the ardent tenderness and I can feel the warm white light embracing our hearts and filling the space around us. When we separate, we both smile and I'm amazed to see that the bruises and cuts all over his face and lips are nearly healed.

He holds up his arms, which are now blessedly pointing in the proper direction, and wiggles his fingers. "Nearly back to normal," he says, "all it took was your kiss."

Alenna clears her throat behind us. "I'll go see Edwin and tell him what happened," she says, breaking the moment, "unless you need me here."

He shakes his head and reaches out for her to come closer. "Thanks, Alenna," he says as he squeezes her hand.

"I'm glad you're okay," she says with a nod.

I walk her to the door. "Thank you," I say, "for being here. And for protecting me."

She nods.

"The truth is," she says grimly as she turns to go, "it's going to take a lot more than me to protect you from Avestan."

Chapter Eighteen

"Are you really healed?" I ask Alexander when I return to him on the couch.

"Almost," he says and then he groans a little as he adjusts his position. "Well, maybe 62 percent … enough for you to climb up on this couch with me."

I smile and snuggle next to him in the space he provided. "Was it really my kiss that helped?"

"I can't think of any other way to explain it."

"You didn't heal yourself?"

"I'm working on it," he says, "but it would have taken me at least a day to get to the state I'm in now, I imagine, without your help."

"Did you know kissing me would heal you?"

"Not at all," he says, shaking his head. "I just wanted to kiss you to kiss you."

I smile. "Then why didn't you look surprised when your arms weren't poking out anymore?"

He chuckles and lets out a groan. "I've ceased to be surprised by anything you can do."

I look up at him. "I told you," he adds, "you're more powerful than you think."

"How did you get to my house?"

"Through normal operations."

"Normal operations? Meaning you walked? On broken legs?"

"Partly."

"Are you serious?"

"I have a high tolerance for pain," he says, "… and a strong desire to be with you."

I shake my head and touch his cheek. "Why did you put yourself in danger like that?"

"He threatened you. I couldn't let it stand."

"But you'd been light traveling all day. You were weakened."

"Alenna told you?"

I nod.

"It doesn't matter. It's handled."

"You could have been killed."

"I gave Avestan a taste of what he's been wanting. He's been back for weeks now, it was inevitable. It's probably a good thing, in retrospect."

"A *good* thing?"

"Like releasing a pressure valve."

"Would you stop talking about it so nonchalantly?" I push his arm in frustration.

"Ow," he wails, recoiling, "62 percent, remember?"

"Oh my God, I'm sorry. I'm so sorry … I forgot. Is this better?" I reposition myself to give him more space between us.

"Actually, I think it would be better if you put your leg over here," he says, pointing to his other side.

"What? You mean like this?" I gently angle my leg across him.

"Yes, and put your right arm over here," he says, pointing again.

"Like this?" I ask, confused, as I lay my arm over him.

He nods. "Okay, now shift a little so that your other knee and arm are along this side. Right here and here," he points.

I start to move as he requested and then I realize what he's doing. I shake my head with a knowing smile and very gingerly climb astride him. "Like this?" I say wryly.

He flashes a wicked smile with a glint in his eyes. "That's it," he says. "Now ease down here—gently mind you—and heal me some more."

We both chuckle as he reaches up and cradles my face, bringing me in slowly for a very tender, very careful kiss.

Chapter Nineteen

I wake up next to Alexander on the couch. He emits a groan when I raise my arm from across his chest.

"Don't move," he orders.

I freeze. "Why? Am I hurting you?"

"No, I just don't want you to go."

I look up at him in disbelief. "I thought I *hurt* you. You're insufferable."

The corners of his mouth upturn in a slow, easy smile. "Good morning to you, too."

I shake my head with a begrudging smile in return. "Morning. I'm going to the bathroom. I'll be right back." I carefully extricate myself to take care of Mother Nature and splash some water on my face. We must have fallen asleep last night in each other's arms. I hardly remember. As I stare at my reflection in the mirror over the sink, I note that my eyes are clear and bright and I realize that last night was the most peaceful, contented rest I've had in weeks.

I return to find Alexander sitting up, stretching. He looks remarkably well, too.

"How do you feel?" I ask.

"Phenomenal, considering."

"What percent is 'phenomenal, considering'?"

He smiles. "82 percent."

I nod, satisfied. "Are you going to tell me what happened?"

"I think it's pretty obvious. I found Avestan and we beat each other senseless."

"Will you stop making jokes about this?"

"It's what happened. And I found out something important: He's not up to full strength yet."

"He isn't? So the fight wasn't too bad?"

He laughs. "Well, it was no picnic, as you could tell by the way I showed up on your doorstep, but he's definitely still recovering from how we left him in Nusquam. No wonder he stayed away this long."

I nod, remembering. I wish he could have remained in Nusquam forever.

"Now," he says, "tell me exactly what happened in the car park yesterday."

I relay the story of Avestan approaching me in the parking lot at Fields and Morris and Justin coming out at the right moment and refusing to leave until Avestan backed off. For some reason I leave out the part about the connection Avestan mentioned between us.

"You told him you think he's *afraid* of you?" Alexander asks.

I nod. "I don't know why, it just came out."

"It came out because it's true. I'm glad you're realizing the power you hold."

"You think so?"

He nods. "Yes, you must have felt it … even through that thick black morass he wears like a shroud. Why else would you have poked that tiger when you were standing there, terrified?"

I can't help but laugh. "That's a good way of putting it. Either that or I'm an idiot."

"You could never be an idiot," Alexander says with a chuckle. "And Justin's a good man, by the way. To sense you were in trouble, come out to help, and stand his ground."

"He *is* a good guy," I say, "but I was terrified Avestan was going to hurt him."

Alexander shakes his head. "Brave, selfless acts carry the power to restore the balance between dark energy and light. Justin followed his instincts and it would have been difficult in that moment for Avestan to channel energy against him."

I'm relieved by what he says. "Will you make sure a guardian watches out for Justin, though, just in case?"

"Of course."

I look into Alexander's eyes, hesitating. I open my mouth to speak and then close it.

"What is it?" he says.

"There's something I want to ask you."

"You know you can ask me anything."

"Okay," I say, "is there something you've been keeping from me?"

"What do you mean?"

"About some connection I have to Avestan?"

"Did he say that?"

"He says you're withholding information." I relay exactly what Avestan said to me and, unless Alexander is a world-class actor, he appears to be as bewildered as I was.

"Edwin and I suspected there was something behind the way Avestan targeted you."

I search his eyes. "So there's something you're not telling me?"

"No. We haven't found anything. And Avestan could be making it up, trying to sow doubt and split us apart."

I nod but don't say anything. That's the thing about pernicious lies—whether they're true or not doesn't matter. Once the seeds of doubt are planted they've already done their damage. Here I am, a small part of me doubting Alexander, even though I know he'd never lie to me.

"Declan," he says, meeting my eyes, "I would tell you."

I nod. "I know," I say. "I know you wouldn't keep something like that from me." I decide to change the subject. "Why were you traveling by light yesterday?"

"I was getting things ready."

"For our plan?"

"Yes."

"Is it still ready?"

"82 percent ready."

I smile. "Are you in a lot of pain?" I ask, concerned.

"Nothing I can't handle."

We sit in silence for a moment. "I don't need any big plan, you know."

"I know," he says. "Something you mentioned once sparked my initial idea but I actually considered changing the whole plan because of something else you said the other day."

"What did I say?"

"If I tell you, it might ruin the surprise."

"Do I get a choice?"

"Of course," he says. "Have I spun this up too much? Would you rather plan it instead?"

I look into his eyes and the caring in their depths touches my heart. "No," I say, "I like how you plan things. And how much thought you put into them. And all the anticipation. But I want you to know I don't need something extravagant. All I care about is me and you. And I think I'm just … impatient."

He smiles. "I love that you're impatient," he says, holding my gaze. "The plan was never extravagant, I promise … in cost, anyway. That wouldn't be us. It will just be you and me and somewhere special when the time is right. But not now, not today, when Avestan is on our minds."

"And you're in pain," I say softly. "I know. I *hate* him. I hate what he does to us. The way he makes me feel, so heavy … and hopeless. Compared to the way I feel when I'm around you, it makes me want to cry."

Alexander caresses my cheek and guides the errant lock of hair that has fallen over my eyes back behind my ear. He kisses me softly. "I'm here," he murmurs, "I'm okay."

I nod and close my eyes, basking in his energy.

"The good news is, Avestan may have just handed us the key to our plan … our *other* plan."

"What do you mean?"

"He wanted to cause a rift between us … let's not disappoint him."

Chapter Twenty

"What rift?" I ask.

"Avestan told you I was keeping something from you—something important that he's willing to tell you and I'm not. He's expecting we'll quarrel over it. He wants you to doubt me. If two people don't trust each other they can't stay together. It's that simple."

"How does this help us?"

"It gives us a plausible reason to break up in his eyes. A reason for me to leave."

"*Now?*" I ask, my heart sinking in my chest.

"The sooner the better. Avestan will expect we've been having a row all night."

"But you're only 82 percent healed."

"I know a way you can help me fix that," he says with that familiar glint.

I push his arm lightly. "How could he expect I'd argue with you when you came here bloody and hurt?"

"He'll assume you're cross with me for putting myself in danger."

"I *am* cross with you for putting yourself in danger."

"See? Not so far-fetched."

I shake my head. "I don't like this idea."

"I was worried he wouldn't follow me when I left—that he wouldn't believe anything could come between us and he'd think I wouldn't stay away. But now I think he's handed us a gift. It could work."

"But what will I tell everyone else why we broke up? And where will I say you went?"

"Edwin can tell everyone I went back to Sydney to visit relatives. Avestan will assume that you don't trust me and that's why we broke up and I left. As far as what you tell everyone else, I'm sure you can come up with plenty of reasons to be rid of me."

I look at him. I know he's joking but it hurts to be so cavalier. "No," I say. "I can't."

"C'mon. We have to make this seem real. Right now Avestan thinks we're in here having a row—that you don't trust me anymore. Tonight I'm going to have to leave and you'll have to look upset."

"I won't have to *look* upset, Alexander, I'll *be* upset," I say with emotion. "I don't want you to go."

"I know," he says, taking my hands, "nor do I. But this is our chance if we can make it believable. What are you going to say to Liz and Finn when they ask why we broke up?"

I shake my head. "I don't know. Your terrible jokes," I say wryly, "how's that?"

Alexander smiles. "I thought you thought I was funny."

"I do," I say petulantly, "I can't come up with anything. I don't want to break up."

"C'mon, we have to do this. What do I do that annoys you?"

"Nothing."

"C'mon."

"Okay … you always have a plan."

He smiles again. "That *annoys* you?"

"Only when you don't share them with me."

"I'm sharing now," he says. "That's why we're having this conversation about stupid pretend reasons to break up."

I smile. "I know."

"So, what else ya got?" he asks wryly.

I meet his eyes. "What am I supposed to say? I can't exactly tell people that you're a guardian angel and you're going to stay young forever and I'm going to get old and decrepit and we can never really work together long term."

He's quiet for a moment. "Is that truly how you feel?"

"No," I say quietly. "Well … sometimes."

"But—"

"I know, I know, age doesn't matter and so on and all that."

"It doesn't."

"What if we have kids?"

"Guardians can't extend the line in that way."

"I know I can't get pregnant, but we could adopt."

"Is that what you want?" he asks.

"Who knows? Maybe someday."

"Then we can adopt."

"How would we explain to a child that their father never ages?"

Alexander meets my eyes and holds my gaze for a long time. "This doesn't feel pretend anymore," he says.

"No," I insist, realizing what I've done, "it is. I don't know why I said any of that. You forced me to come up with something and—"

"I never realized so clearly that you'd be better off with a mortal."

"What? What are you talking about? I only want to be with you."

"But you could have a normal life," he says. "With kids and a husband who grows old."

"Who says I want a normal life? I want to be with you." I look into his eyes, pleading for him to understand. "We're just pretending. None of this is real."

He remains silent.

"Maybe it'll be good for me to be away for a while," he says finally.

"No," I say, shaking my head, "it won't. Because I love you."

He looks up at me. "I love you, too … I love you enough to do what's best."

"Alexander," I cry, "no, I don't want to do this anymore. We're not breaking up. You're not leaving!" My voice is hoarse and I wrap my arms around him and kiss him with all the urgency and love in my heart.

At first he doesn't respond. He stays rigidly still, holding me by the arms but not pushing me away. I'm careful, so I won't hurt him, but I persist, kissing him again until I feel him relenting. I tug at his bottom lip and his lips finally part and my tongue finds his. He moans deep in his throat and flips us over until I'm beneath him on the couch. He kisses me hard, with abandon, and I glide my hands along his skin and over the granite muscles of his chest and slide his shirt off, over his head. His mouth comes down on mine again and he cups my breasts, massaging them through the thin fabric of my blouse before unbuttoning one button and then tearing it open the rest of the way in his haste and sliding it off me. His eyes are ablaze and I unzip my skirt and push it down until I'm left in just my bra and panties as we continue to kiss with wild, primal intensity. My hands drift down, low on his hips, to his jeans where we both tug to undo them and slide them off with force. He strains against his boxer briefs and I wrap my legs around him as we kiss until I can feel his length pushing against me. I reach down to slide off my panties and Alexander pushes off his briefs and then, as I feel him pressing against me, my body aching for him, he lets out a low, hoarse growl from deep within his throat and rolls off to lie on his back beside me on the couch.

"Did I hurt you?" I breathe.

"No," he groans, breathing hard. "We can't do this. Not like this."

"I want to," I breathe as I shift to my side, "and I know you do, too." My eyes trail over his sculpted chest and abs, straying lower to the evidence before me.

He groans, hesitating, raking his fingers through his thick, dark hair. "No," he says finally. He sits up and reaches for his briefs. "This isn't how it should be."

"I don't care how it should be," I say. "I love you. I want to make love to you."

He turns to face me. "That wasn't making love. It was hot and raw and out of control."

"What's wrong with hot, raw sex?"

I see him trying to hold back a smile but a trace appears anyway at the corner of his mouth. "Nothing," he says. "I plan for us to have plenty of it. But not for your first time. Not for *our* first time."

"That's one of your plans? To have hot, raw sex with me?"

Both corners of his mouth are now clearly invoked in his smile. "I *hope* to," he says. "As well as romantic sex, and fun, playful sex, and deeply intimate sex. If you want to." His expression turns serious. "But not now. Not when we're doing it because we're breaking things off."

"But we're just pretending to break things off."

Alexander is silent.

"Right?"

He still doesn't answer.

"Alexander," I say, sitting up, "I'm not going along with this plan if you don't agree."

He slides over closer and takes my hands. "Declan, I love you. Always. But we need to make this real … so Avestan will follow me and leave you safe, okay?"

"But it's not real …"

He hesitates before answering. "I'll always love you. That's real."

I stare at him, silently.

"If you'd rather be free while I'm gone," he adds, "I understand. And maybe that's best … to consider yourself free."

"Free?"

"To date other people. Mortals."

Tears well up in my eyes. "No," I say, shaking my head. "Please, Alexander, don't do this. Don't say that."

He pulls me toward him and kisses my tears away, one at a time. "It will be okay," he whispers.

"How will you going away ever be okay?" I ask bitterly. "Will I even hear from you?"

"We shouldn't communicate," he says. "Avestan needs to think we're through. But if you absolutely have to reach me, get word through Edwin."

"How long will you be gone?"

"As long as it takes for Avestan to follow me and for me to defeat him, away from here."

My tears are flowing steadily now and my eyes plead with Alexander to reconsider.

He gently sweeps a stray lock of hair from my eyes and tucks it behind my ear. "I don't want to spend our last day together having a row," he says softly.

"Our last day? Alexander, you're scaring me."

"Only for a while."

His eyes are endless pools and I stare into them sadly, knowing there's nothing I can say that will ever change his mind. "Just hold me," I say softly as he pulls me in close against him and I feel the warmth of his body for what I achingly pray isn't the last time.

Chapter Twenty-One

The first day was the easiest, in retrospect.

With each day Alexander continues to be gone, without any word, my worry grows and festers. He was still injured when he left. *Why didn't he wait?* What if Avestan went after him again right away? I miss him profoundly. It's only been a little over a week since he left but it might as well be a year. Each day I don't think I can feel any worse yet I do. I trudge through the motions of my normal routine but inside I'm so worried about Alexander I can hardly focus. I'm determined not to sit around and ruminate over where he is and what he's doing every minute while he's gone but it's not easy. My inner drill sergeant yells at me regularly to stop being such a wuss. Just because Alexander's gone it doesn't mean I'm helpless for Pete's sake. I have powers … and I can make things happen, too. Maybe *I* can be the one to end this once and for all. I pump myself up like this regularly only to review the situation again and fall into despair. Avestan is a dark angel powerful enough to kill Alexander. How could I ever defeat him as a freaking sprite? Up and down I go with my emotions and when I'm down I force myself to get back up and go to work and hang out with friends and distract myself from missing him and worrying about him endlessly or I'll go crazy. I really will.

Before he left I made him tell me all the things we'll do when he comes back. I looked into his eyes as he recited each one because in my heart of hearts I'm not sure that he's planning to. I'm holding onto the idea that he wants me to be unsure, on purpose, so my heartache appears more real. But it *is* real. The hardest part hasn't been convincing everyone we broke up for good—that's evident to anyone with eyes. The hardest part has been maintaining the guise that Alexander and

I both chose to end it, and that I'm okay with this. And the cherry topping on this rotten sundae is that the plan doesn't even seem to be working. Avestan left San Mar after his fight with Alexander, but two days ago, according to Alenna, he came back.

"Declan! Finn!" Mrs. Warner says when she opens the door to Liz's house. "How nice to see you. I'm sorry though, dears—Liz is at work right now. She isn't here."

"Hi Fran," we say, calling Mrs. Warner by her first name, which she vehemently prefers. "Nice to see you, too," I say. "We actually know Liz isn't here but we came by because I think I left my phone here the last time I was over. Do you mind if we take a look?"

"Of course," she says with a welcome smile as she opens the door wide and steps aside to let us in.

"Finn," I say, "do you think it's in the family room? Is that where you thought you saw me leave it?" Finn nods with vigor but doesn't answer. He doesn't want to be embarrassed by admitting that he lost Liz's present, but he can't lie to Mrs. Warner. Or anyone else. Even white lies. He'd just stumble all over himself trying to do it and be obvious—like the strange way he's nodding right now. It's simply not in his nature to tell an untruth. He took a job at the boardwalk one summer working the game where you throw three balls to try to break a bunch of plastic plates lined up in rows in the back of the booth. If you broke one or two you'd get a tiny prize like a small stuffed crab or a blow-up mallet with the "San Mar Boardwalk" logo stamped on it, but if you managed to break a plate all three times, you got to choose one of the impressively enormous stuffed animals hanging along the walls of the booth. Invariably he'd get guys who were trying to impress their girlfriends (who were clearly coveting one of the big prizes) and, after expending many rounds of cash, they'd say something like, "*C'mon,* I've broken two every round, this game is rigged, just give it to me." I told Finn the best way to defuse those situations was to say, "I would if I could, but it's against the rules and I'll get in trouble," to take the heat off of him and put it on a faceless bureaucracy. But Finn couldn't lie—he *wouldn't* give them the big prize if it was up to him, because they didn't meet the full criteria (set by his bosses and clearly stated to Finn when he was trained) for a "large win." Instead, he insisted on saying, "I'm sorry sir, but the rules clearly state that you have to break a plate with all three throws. You didn't manage to do that. But if you think you can succeed, you're welcome to keep trying." I was afraid some drunk guy was going to end up punching him someday. At any rate, that leaves me in charge of the fib-telling to Mrs. Warner right now, so we can get to work tearing Liz's house apart to find the ring he hid here. Somewhere.

"You have free rein of the house to search," Mrs. Warner says cheerily, spreading her arms wide, "but I'm sorry I can't help. I'm hosting my weekly drawing class in the back yard right now. Feel free to join the class after you find your phone if you're interested. It's quite fun. A lively group."

Finn and I smile and thank her. I can't help wondering what 'a lively group' means in Mrs. Warner parlance because she's a pretty lively lady all on her own. I like Mrs. Warner. A lot. Liz pretends to be embarrassed by her sometimes, and maybe she is … but not really. Her mom is cool, like almost too cool. Liz and I have so many good stories involving her mom's artsy eccentricity through the years that we laugh so hard we cry and practically pee our pants when we play them back for each other.

As soon as Mrs. Warner leaves, Finn and I go to the family room and get to work searching on opposite sides. It's a big space with a game table and chairs, large couches in the middle, bookshelves lining the outside walls, and an entertainment center at one end with more shelves holding a large collection of original vinyl albums, among other things.

"I'm sorry," Finn says after about forty minutes of fruitless searching.

"Finn, don't worry about it," I say, "we all lose things. It's not a big deal, and we'll find it."

"But we've been looking for a long time. And the anniversary is tomorrow."

He's right. We've been looking for a while, and in about forty minutes more we'll have to leave because we're meeting Liz downtown. As we've been searching I've been lamenting the fact (strictly in mind only) that Finn didn't buy Liz a giant present, like a stuffed animal or a bike, rather than something tiny like a ring that is proving freaking impossible to find. "It's okay," I say with forced calmness, "it didn't disappear. It's here. We'll find it. Maybe if we take a break for a second it'll help. Do you want a glass of water?" I realize as I say the words that my throat is parched.

"No, I want to keep looking," he says as he pulls another book off the bookshelf he's been searching through.

"Okay, you keep going and I'll be right back," I say. "I'm dying of thirst."

I walk into the kitchen and try my damnedest to shove the image of Mr. and Mrs. Warner in here with ice cubes and a spatula out of my mind as I grab a glass from the cupboard. *Why in God's name did Liz have to tell me that?* I get some ice from the freezer, and then turn to the kitchen sink for some water. I decide to take a peek out the window at Mrs. Warner's "lively" drawing class in the back yard to see what it's all about as I wait for the water from the tap to fill my glass. I scan the large yard over to the pool area and see a group of about seven ladies sitting on stools in front of easels with pencils, sketching. As I continue to scan the scene my eyes nearly pop out of my skull at the vision of a very buff, very nude, very *well-endowed* man posing provocatively on a white lounge chair in front of them. Mrs. Warner and the other ladies are sketching furiously and I can hear trills of merry conversation as they go about their work. *Jesus,* I should have known not to look … Mrs. Warner is the woman who told Liz and me when we were twelve that she was taking us up the coast to a "naturists" beach—something that also sounded harmless (*and fun!*) at the time but also popped the eyes out of my skull in the end.

"Are you sure you hid it here, in the family room?" I ask Finn when I get back.

He nods. "Or somewhere in the theatre downstairs."

"Why didn't you hide it in her bedroom?"

"I didn't want her to find it."

"But what if her mom or dad found it?"

He pauses from pulling out books stacked on the large walnut bookshelf. "It's not their anniversary. It wouldn't ruin the surprise."

I stop opening and closing drawers. "It's in a box, right?"

Finn looks at me, puzzled.

"A ring box?"

"If a ring box is a clear plastic bag with a zipper."

"It's in a Ziploc bag?"

"A miniature one," he says, "the size of a movie ticket."

My eyes go wide at the thought of how much harder it will be to find a ring in a tiny plastic bag, but I try not to show alarm.

"That's how they sold it to me," he explains.

"That's fine," I say with as much nonchalance as I can muster. "I just need to know what form factor we're looking for."

"Oh. The form factor is a card," he says.

"You put the ring bag in a card?"

"Yes. An anniversary card."

I groan inside because I haven't been looking for a card, but I keep it together. I don't want to upset Finn. It's my fault for not clarifying all this earlier. "Okay," I say. "Is the envelope white?"

"It's dark pink."

"With Liz's name on it?"

He nods. My shoulders slump with relief. *Thank God.* I would have noticed a pink envelope with Finn's writing. I won't have to re-search covered territory. "That's good," I say. "If Liz found it, she wouldn't open it. She'd call you first."

Finn visibly relaxes for the first time since we got here and when I see how tensed up he was my heart hurts for him. He did all the right things buying this present for Liz and now he thinks he messed it up.

He places a stack of books back on the shelf. "What if we don't find it?"

"We won't stop until we do," I say with determination as I start looking through the Warners' collection of vinyl record albums one by one. Twenty tedious minutes later a pink envelope with "To Liz" written on it sails to the floor when I pull out Led Zeppelin's album *In Through The Out Door*.

"Found it!" I cry out as I pat the envelope and feel a blessedly tell-tale lump.

Finn turns and peers at the album in my hand. "Oh yeah," he says, "I remember now."

I shake my head and smile. "Do you want to take it home with you?"

"No, put it back. Otherwise I might forget to bring it over tomorrow."

I shake my head again and slide it back in front of the album. I can't argue with his logic. And, at least now, two of us know where it is.

As Finn and I walk to meet Liz downtown my mind wanders as we talk and eventually lands where it always does, on Alexander. I close my eyes for a moment and imagine sending the warm white light in my core to him wherever he is to keep him safe. It calms me to imagine that I have a modicum of control over the situation and I take a deep breath in and try to set all my worries aside for the night so I can focus on this evening with Finn and Liz.

On our way, we stop at Finn's house. His parents are at a work conference and Finn needs to feed Zeno, his dog. The day Finn and I met in pre-K we rescued Zeno when he was just a little beagle-mix puppy. I was jealous when Finn got to keep him but I consider Zeno my dog, too, and so does Finn. We spent many a day playing with Zeno for hours and then eating peanut butter sandwiches (Finn's plain, mine with jelly) and drinking homemade lemonade at the picnic table in his back yard. Zeno has a favorite spot where he likes to sit under the poplar tree in the back corner of the fence and I suspect he likes the way the wind sounds rustling through its leaves as much as I do. It's peaceful … and relaxing. I always loved coming to Finn's house.

We open the side gate to enter through the back yard and I smile when I see our old picnic table and Zeno sitting in his spot under the tree. He jumps up when he sees us and walks over so we can pet him. He's gotten slower over the years but he's still as cheerful and loving. He rolls over on his back so we can rub his tummy and then he pops up again and walks through the doggy door and peers at us through the sliding glass door in back of the house, waiting for us to join him inside.

When Finn walks up to the door to unlock it Zeno licks the glass and then he plops his long tongue out of the side of his mouth and lets it hang there, hysterically. When we laugh, he does it again, flattening his tongue against the clear glass as he licks it, and then letting his long tongue fall out of his mouth to the side, hanging like a limp necktie. It's so funny and the more he does it the more we laugh until Finn and I both have tears in our eyes from laughing so hard. God, I love Zeno. Somehow he knew to cheer me up and take my mind off Alexander right when I needed it.

When we reach Surf Pizza downtown and step up to join the line extending outside to the sidewalk, Finn peers over at me. "You look kind of awful," he says.

I meet his eyes. Finn can be very observant when he wants to—he once memorized the rotation of our gym teacher Mr. Finkle's wardrobe—and he's also very, very blunt. "Gee, thanks Finn."

He looks guilty. "I shouldn't have said that."

"It's okay," I say. "You're only telling the truth. I *do* look terrible. I haven't slept much and I was thinking about Alexander."

"I don't understand you," he says.

"Why?"

"Why did you break up with him if it's making you miserable?"

"It was never going to work."

"Why?"

"Eventually he'd be going back to Australia for good."

"But when?"

I wonder if he's purposely trying to irritate me but I can see by his eyes and his tone that he's genuinely just trying to understand. "I don't know, Finn, but eventually … and it would hurt too much. It was a mutual decision—we broke up with each other."

"Then why are you so sad?"

"Because I miss him."

"Then why did you break up with him?"

I put my face in my palms and stare at him through my fingers as I drag my hands down my cheeks. "Finn," I growl, "I know you want an answer that makes sense. But I don't have one. Sometimes you have to do things you don't want to do because they're the right decision. In the long run."

Finn is silent.

"I'm sorry," I say, "I didn't mean to snap at you."

He nods. "I'm just sorry you're sad."

Something in the way he goes straight to how I'm feeling makes my eyes tear up. "Thanks, Finn," I say, squeezing his hand. "I'll be okay."

I look around again for Liz as we move forward a little in line but still don't see her.

"Can I ask you something?" I say.

"Sure."

"You know that list you keep in your head of all the things to worry about? Alphabetized?"

"Yes," he adds.

"What do you do when you *don't* want to think about those things?" I ask. "How do you turn it off?"

"Why would I want to do that?"

"So you don't worry all the time."

"That's the reason I keep the list. The statistical chances of most bad things happening are very low. Especially if you take common sense precautions."

"So, you like it," I say, "because it helps you keep things in perspective."

He nods.

"So what do you recommend I do if I don't want to think about something? And I don't want to keep a list in my head of probabilities?"

He thinks for a moment before answering. "Drink barbecue sauce."

"*What?*"

"It seems like it would taste good, but it doesn't."

I laugh. "Are you serious?"

"You won't be able to think about anything else for a while, because you'll be trying to get the taste out of your mouth."

"Did you *do* that?" I ask. I'm weirdly fascinated by this conversation.

"Once."

"Why?"

"I like my mom's barbecued chicken. Then I wasn't eating meat anymore so I figured I'd cut out the middle man and just drink the sauce."

I can't help but laugh. "How much did you drink?"

"I realized quickly it was a bad idea." He looks at me and we both start to laugh.

"Did you get sick?"

He shakes his head. "You know me."

I nod. Finn loves spicy things. He eats jalapenos whole and he loves big gobs of wasabi with his sushi. The guy craves intense flavor and he has an iron stomach. Yet, for whatever reason, he recoils from eating all fruit as if it's poison.

"I don't think I want to drink barbecue sauce," I say.

Finn shrugs. "You could also do math problems in your head. I used to do that when you had panic attacks. Before you told me to hold your hand. Actually, now I do both. Sometimes. But you haven't had any lately."

I smile at him. I don't know what I would have done without Finn in my life.

"Or you could watch cat videos on YouTube," Liz says as she walks up.

"Huh?" I say as I turn to give her a hug hello.

"I heard you guys talking," she says. "YouTube is the answer. Remember that video we made of Willow dressed like a leprechaun?"

We all laugh.

"We should make some more of those," she says. "We haven't done any in a long time."

I smile. "I don't know if Willow would let us dress her up anymore," I say. "She mostly just likes to sit in my lap these days."

We reach the front of the line and order our pizza slices and drinks.

"Are you trying to distract yourself from Alexander?" Liz asks as we sit down in a booth with our food.

I nod, knowing she understands.

"That's what we're here for," she says. "Like right now, making you celebrate our seven-month anniversary a day early, at my favorite pizza place in the entire freaking world." She takes a bite of her 'Veggie Special' slice and groans. "This is amazeballs."

I smile. "Do you want your present now since you and Finn are going down to Moonstone Beach tomorrow?"

"You got us a present?" she says. "Are you kidding? You didn't have to do that. You're the one who got us together."

"So you don't want it then?" I tease.

She tilts her head and smiles. "Hand it over."

I laugh and bend down to get it out of the bag by my feet.

"This present idea must be making the rounds," Liz says as I slide my gift to her across the table. "My mom heard me talking about our anniversary with Finn and she says she has something for us, too. Probably because she likes Finn so much." She flashes a smile in his direction. "I think it's a gift certificate to that new vegan restaurant that just opened up. I *hope.* I don't think she'd have time to give us anything too crazy. She's working on some big art project." Her voice lowers a register before she continues. "The model she's painting is seriously *hung,* you should see it."

I laugh. I can't tell her that I think I just *did* see it when we were searching her house.

You sure you don't want to come with us tomorrow?" she asks.

"Are you nuts?" I say. "Tomorrow is for you guys. I've got some things planned with my mom anyway."

Liz unties the bow on the flat, rectangular package and unwraps the fuchsia tissue paper to uncover a framed picture of her and Finn. She stares at it for a long time and I can see the emotion in her eyes when she looks up. "Where'd you find this?" she asks.

"I was organizing some old photos and when I saw it I knew I wanted to give it to you."

The photo is of her and Finn at the river in Basin Park when we were in eighth grade. We used to go there all the time and swing off a rope somebody hung from a branch that stretches out over the water. In the photo they're dripping wet in their swimsuits, standing on the bank of the river. Finn is looking very cute and leanly muscular with his floppy brown hair and boyish face, and Liz is next to him. They have their arms around each other. Liz is smiling at the camera, laughing, and Finn is smiling, too, but he's beaming up at Liz (who back then, before Finn's growth spurt, was far more than just a quarter inch taller than him). The look in his eyes is unmistakable. He loved Liz even back then. Probably before he even realized it. I knew Liz would see it, too.

Finn peers over Liz's shoulder at the photo. "Your thumb is in the corner," he says to me.

I nod. "I thought of cropping that out but then I thought it was a funny way for me to be in the photo, too. I used to love it when we all went out to the river. Do you remember blowing up all those inner tubes?"

"I wasn't looking at the camera," Finn adds.

"That's because you were looking at me," Liz pipes in. "Which was nice," she adds, "and I love it." She gives him a kiss.

"Thank you," Liz says to me, meeting my eyes with emotion.

"You're welcome," I smile. "That was a good day."

"It was," Liz says nostalgically. "We had a lot of good days there."

We all smile and sigh for a moment, remembering, and then we toast with our fountain drinks and I dive into the delicious thin crust slice before me. As I savor the perfect ratio of marinara, mozzarella, and dough I realize that for ten straight minutes I managed not to worry about Alexander.

One more reason I cherish my friends.

Chapter Twenty-Two

"Why, exactly, are we going bowling?" I ask my mom as she drives us to the Surf Bowl. I've been so busy all summer we haven't been able to spend much time together and I miss just hanging out. That's what we're doing tonight.

"I don't know, it's something different," she replies. "I thought about miniature golf but we just did that after your graduation, and I considered a movie but you said there's nothing good out. I saw a Groupon for this place and we haven't been bowling since you were a kid. And, as I remember, we were both terrible bowlers," she laughs. "This should be fun."

I can't help but return her goofy smile. She's right. I didn't want to go to a movie because the only good ones out right now are romances. That's the last thing I need thrust in my face.

When we arrive, I see a group of guys and a girl in the corner of the parking lot, dressed all in black. They remind me of Avestan and a shiver runs up my spine. *Could they be dark angels?* I stare over at them and the girl looks up at me and glares. *Probably because you're staring at her, Declan.* I hate this not knowing and wondering all the time who are the good guys and bad guys. I almost wish Alenna didn't warn me that Avestan is back. Edwin said that whenever Avestan is away a lot of the dark angels in San Mar leave to pursue easier, lower hanging fruit somewhere else, where there aren't so many guardians around. Turns out dark guardians are lazy. What a surprise.

My mom puts her arm around me and pulls me in for a quick hug against her side as we walk into the Surf Bowl. I can tell she's excited and I'm surprised at how busy it is inside. There's a long row of alleys and rock music is playing over the rhythmic sounds of bowling balls thudding onto the smooth, polished wood and smashing and scattering pins. The young girl at the counter tells us the wait will be about an hour at the same time Chief Stephens spots us and walks over.

"Hi Judy, hey Declan, you ladies here to bowl?" he asks with a smile. He's dressed casually, out of his police chief uniform, and he has a bowling ball in his hand.

My mom looks startled. "Hi Mark. Yes, we just got here. We're waiting for a lane to open up."

"Would you like to join us?" he asks. "I'm here with my boys. They're home for the summer. You remember Jake and Zach, don't you Declan?"

I nod. "Of course." Jake and Zach are a couple years older than me but we all used to play as kids. Their mom used to make the best chocolate milk and brownies. I always loved going to their house. When Mrs. Stephens died of cancer years ago it was a loss the whole town felt. She was such a nice lady. For about the last twelve months I suspected Chief Stephens had a thing for my mom and she must have finally given him a sign she was ready because he asked her out for coffee a couple months ago and she accepted. They've been dating—I think—ever since. I haven't been able to get much information out of her. She insists they're just friends.

"So would you like to join us?" he asks again.

My mom looks at me. I can tell she's debating what to do. This was supposed to be our night together. But Chief Stephens is a nice guy. Handsome, too, for an older guy, judging from the way all the single moms in town react to him. As much as I miss my dad, I want my mom to keep living and be happy. She could use a little fun.

"Sure," I say. "Thanks, Chief."

"You know you can call me Mark," he says with a grin.

I smile. "Habit."

My mom turns to me. "Are you sure?" she asks in a hushed whisper.

"Yes, it'll be fun," I whisper back, nudging her.

She turns back and smiles at Mark. "Declan and I haven't bowled in years. We're probably not much competition."

"If you were any good I may have to rescind my offer. My boys and I are terrible," he says with a laugh. "We came here on a whim, just looking for something different to do. I bought a Groupon."

My mom looks at me and I can tell her mind is spinning with the wonders of coincidence and fate.

"Same with us," I say.

"Great," he declares, "it was meant to be. Declan, we're on lane fourteen over there." He points in the direction of the lane and waves to try to get his sons' attention. "Jake and Zach can help you get situated. I'm searching for a heavier ball," he says, lifting the bowling ball stuck to his hand. "Judy, do you want to come with me and I can help you find a good one, too?"

I walk over to lane fourteen and tap on Zach's shoulder.

He turns around and his eyes widen with recognition and surprise. "Declan Jane?" he says. "Look at you, all grown up."

Jake turns and smiles, too, when he sees me. "The years have been good to you," he says.

I laugh and give them both hugs. "You, too. My mom and I came here to bowl on a whim and we ran into your dad over there." I tilt my head in the direction of the chief and my mom. "He asked us to join you guys."

"So your mom and our dad, huh?" Zach says conspiratorially.

I nod. "I know. You guys okay with that?"

"Okay?" Zach says. "We're not only okay, we're fully on board. Dad needs some fun in his life again. And your mom was always one of the nicest moms in the neighborhood."

"She always had popsicles," says Jake.

"And she'd save me a grape," says Zach, "which is still my favorite flavor. Does she have any popsicles on her tonight?"

I laugh.

"How do *you* feel about it?" Jake asks me.

I shrug. "Same as you guys. My mom could use a little fun. And I like your dad."

"Good, so we're all agreed," says Zach. "Our parents are cleared for action. Now let's find you a bowling ball so we can start this game and beat you soundly."

I laugh. "Bring it."

We laugh and joke and have a good time as we bowl for the next two hours but inside thoughts of Alexander are never far away. I can't manage to push away completely the worries that keep resurfacing of Avestan coming after me and Alexander never coming back.

"Did you have fun?" my mom asks as we're driving home.

"Yeah," I answer, surprising myself. "Did you?"

"Yes, but I'm sorry that our night together got hijacked."

"But we had fun," I insist. "We'll have plenty of other nights with just us. This was a nice distraction. Really."

She glances over to meet my eyes. "Good," she says. "How are you doing?"

"I'm okay."

"Are you ever going to tell me more about what happened?"

"There isn't much more to it, other than what I already said. And I honestly don't want to talk about it. Tonight I was finally able to not think about Alexander for a while."

"I really don't understand you two," she says. "I think—"

"Please, mom, I know what you think. And, please, I don't want to talk about it tonight. And speaking of not understanding people, I don't understand why you don't just admit you're dating Chief Stephens."

My mom looks at me, surprised. "I'm not dating Mark."

"What do you mean? You've been out with him a bunch of times."

"We're just friends."

"Friends with benefits?" I ask boldly.

"Declan!" she says. "I couldn't do that to your father."

I search her face. She's serious. I was right. My mom is *not* getting all Willy Wonka Wonderland—or whatever the heck Liz said—with Chief Stephens. She pulls into our driveway and I touch my mom's arm to keep her from exiting the car.

"Mom," I say softly, "dad's gone. It's okay to be with someone else."

She turns to look at me. "I know," she says quietly. "Intellectually, I know that, Declan. But I can't. Not yet. I'm not ready."

"It's been a long time, mom. He would want you to move forward … you know that."

"I know," she says quietly. "Mark is a kind man … and patient. He understands what it is to miss someone. He lost someone he loved deeply, too."

I lean over to hug her and she wraps her arms around me tight. "I love you, honey," she says. "And I worry about you. I want you to be with someone who makes you laugh, and makes your heart sing, and brings out the best in you, like your dad did for me. If that's not Alexander then I understand and I'll stop asking questions."

My eyes well up as I try to speak. "Alexander does all those things, mom," I say quietly with my head on her shoulder.

"But please don't ask anymore," I whisper, and the tears start to fall.

What I don't say—what I can't say—is that I know in my heart I'll never fully recover if Alexander isn't able to defeat Avestan and come back to me.

Chapter Twenty-Three

"I can't believe it," I say, "he's dead."

"Good riddance," Finn says.

"How can you say that?" I ask.

"You were risking your life."

"He was good to me."

"It's not a person, Dec. It's a *car* … an inanimate object." The expression on Finn's face makes me wonder if sometimes he thinks I'm clinically insane.

"But Archie was my first car, Finn. He chugged along for longer than I ever had a right to expect, based on how cheap he was. He got me where I needed to go."

"Yes, but at added statistical risk."

I shrug. "He was a classic."

"Being old doesn't automatically make something a classic," he says. "I'm glad you won't be driving it anymore."

Finn never liked Archie because of the obvious safety limitations of a 1972 VW Bug. No modern seatbelts, no airbags, a tinny-sounding air-cooled engine mounted in the back and myriad other weaknesses professed by Finn, including something about "crumple zones." From the obvious relief evident on his face, I'm reminded of how worried he was about me driving it all this time and that tugs on my heart. *Oh, Finn.* I hug his shoulders.

"I'm sorry you never got to drive him," I say. Finn and I have diligently poured ourselves into his driving lessons but we always use his mom's year-old Mazda, which apparently meets all current safety standards. Finn refused to drive Archie, even in a parking lot.

"I'm not," says Finn.

I smile crookedly. "Well, thanks for coming to get me," I say. I'm grateful Liz and Finn were able to come so quickly. My mom is out showing houses all day and Alenna left two days ago for a quick meet-up with Alexander. To say I've been anxiously awaiting her return for a report on how he's doing is an understatement of mass proportions. Next on my list to call would have been Edwin, but he's been so busy lately. I've seen a lot of cars parked at his house and many late night meetings. Out of acute curiosity I take note whenever I can of who goes in and out. At first I assumed they were all guardians but one day I saw Eddie Garrett, a jerk of a guy two years ahead of me in school, coming out of Edwin's house. There's *no way* that guy's a guardian. He used to call me "midget" and yank my ponytail when we were kids. He must be a university student of Edwin's or something. It's maddening that Edwin and Alenna won't just 'fess up and tell me who all the guardians are.

"I got him up to five hundred," says Liz proudly as she walks out of the service door and joins Finn and me in the parking lot. "And you don't have to pay for the tow."

"Really? I already told him I'd take two fifty."

"Yeah, and I told him you were under the heavy influence of carbon monoxide fumes when you agreed to that highway robbery," she says dismissively. "What the hell happened anyway? Archie won't even start."

"I don't know. I drove over the hill to deliver some papers to the Fields and Morris office in San Jose and when I was coming back I was almost to the summit when Archie started slowing down … so I downshifted and something just blew. I managed to make it to the side of the road and I tried all the things I normally do, like adjusting the throttle, but nothing worked. I knew something big was wrong this time."

"I rescued this from the trunk for you." Liz reveals the gas can she was holding behind her.

I smile. It's the one she gave me as a joke because the gas gauge never worked and I kept running out and getting us stranded. I look at her and Finn and it really hits me that this is *it*. Thanks to Liz, the mechanic that towed me here has agreed to buy Archie for $500 rather than $250, but money is small consolation. I'm feeling pretty choked up, to be honest, like I'm losing an old friend.

"Will you guys take a picture with me in front of Archie before we go?" I ask, swallowing the lump in my throat.

We gather together in front of my cheery-looking yet non-operational bug and my smile is bittersweet as we snap the photo. Liz collects the $500 cash from Tom, the mechanic (who has promised to restore Archie to optimal fighting form) and I hang back for a moment. "Bye, Archie," I say quietly as I trace my hand over the roof. I peer at his crumpled fender with the garish red paint scrape showing beneath the newer layer of canary-yellow paint. "You'll finally get fixed up the way you deserved."

"You did the right thing," Liz says, patting my shoulder as we drive away in her blue Fiat. "It would have cost way too much to rebuild the engine and get him working again."

"I know," I say with a lump in my throat as I look back toward the garage. "It was time … but it still hurts." Liz turns on some music on the car radio and my mind wanders and before I know it she and Finn are dropping me off back at Fields and Morris.

"You need me to pick you up?" Liz asks as I get out. "When your shift is over?"

"No, my mom can pick me up, thanks. I'm babysitting Charlie later, but I can bike there or use my mom's car."

She nods. "Maybe you'll get to see Malibu Barbie."

"God, I hope not. I think she's still in France." Molly has been away for a while visiting her dad in Paris.

"Sorry to break it to you," Liz says, "but she's back. I saw her downtown yesterday."

I groan loudly. "Great, I lost Archie and gained Molly Bing."

Liz laughs. "Your life is a shit show right now."

"Thanks," I say dryly.

"Hey, if we can't laugh about it, we cry." she says. "Things will get better … I promise. And in the meantime you've got five Benjamins." She hands me a stack of crumpled twenties.

"These are Jacksons," I say.

She smiles. "But they *add up* to five Benjamins," she says. "Go stick this in that chewed-up shoebox under your bed you call a bank, but keep a little out and buy yourself something for once. Girls with broken hearts deserve new shoes."

I smile. She's right about the chewed-up part. Willow—my cat who thinks she's a dog—loves to chew up cardboard. She goes at it like crazy and leaves bits and pieces everywhere. "Thanks," I say to Liz, "for everything … and for getting that guy up to five hundred."

"Negotiating is my specialty," she says with a wide grin. She reaches out of the car window and grasps my hand, searching my eyes. "You okay?" she asks.

I nod.

"Call us if you need anything," Liz says.

I nod again and lean down to look through the window to the passenger side so I can see both her and Finn. The loving kindness emanating from the two of them makes me feel like no bad guardians could ever reach me through all this goodness. "Bye you guys, thanks."

When I go back into the Fields and Morris building I find that Justin has left for the day. He said something earlier about his lease being up and he and his roommates having to pack and move. That's why when Mr. Fields rushed into our conference room this morning and asked if one of us could deliver some documents to the San Jose court before noon, I volunteered. Apparently the courier didn't show. I was happy to have something to do other than mindless scanning anyway. I sit down, alone now, in the conference room, ready to resume scanning documents from the file box I started on this morning but as I search around for the open box I was working on I see that it's gone. I look under the table and over near Justin's workspace and it's not there either. Maybe somebody closed it by mistake and put it back in the "to do" stack. I pull up the last-scanned files on my computer to remind myself what the documents were so I can match the year and case to the leftover files. I nod my head, remembering, when I see the files. They were documents from estate cases from over ten years ago and the last one I was working on was for a woman named Esther Winchester. I remember thinking that "Esther" and "chester" rhymed. I open the boxes stacked next to me and flip through the files. They're all from more recent years. Where did the box I was working on go? I place a flag on the file in the system and note that it's incomplete and then I start on a new box. I'll have to ask Justin about it later.

My mom picks me up and when I relay the story about Archie she commiserates but she admits she always hoped I'd get a newer, safer car sooner rather than later. Unfortunately, two complicated real estate transactions she was working on just fell out of escrow before closing, so any help in contributions to the "car fund" department will have to wait. Maybe it's the rawness at the thought of replacing Archie, but when I consider it from a practical standpoint I don't really need a car for now. Between Liz—and soon, Finn—driving, I'll always have a ride. And I can bike or take the bus if I have to. I'll save the money I would have otherwise put toward gas and oil changes. Maybe it's a good thing. Or maybe I'm fooling myself and I inherited my mom's way of searching for a silver lining.

I drive over to Charlie's house at seven in my mom's car and when I see Molly's BMW parked in the driveway my stomach drops. *Ugh.* It was so nice the last few times I've been here when she was gone to France to visit her dad. Memories of Charlie throwing up pepperoni pizza and cherry Slurpee in my face make me shiver in my seat. I hope to God Molly hasn't been in charge of watching him again before I arrived.

I ring the doorbell. When the door opens, Molly is standing there as if she never left, giving me the stink eye. Nice to know Paris hasn't changed her.

"Oh, it's you," she says blandly.

"Hi Molly, you're back."

"No shit, Sherlock," she says as she opens the door wider to let me in.

I stifle a smile. Maybe she gained a sense of humor in Europe. There's a stretch of awkward silence as she watches me take off my shoes in the foyer, so I try to make conversation. "How was Paris?"

"Fine," she says flatly, "as long as I wasn't near my stepmom and step-brats."

I hesitate before asking my next question. I don't want to get overly chummy but I feel obligated to warn her if need be. "Hey," I try to say casually, "I've been meaning to ask, are you still going out with that guy Avestan?" I asked Alexander once how dark guardians can date mortals and he said they make their own rules—love isn't involved and they enjoy mixing with mortals to further their means or simply to cause pain. As much as I don't like Molly, I don't want her caught up in that.

Her eyes narrow. "Why, you jealous?" Before I can answer she adds, "He would never go for you. You're not his type."

I cough and nearly choke, holding back my reaction. *If you only knew.* "So you're not with him anymore?"

"I don't need assholes who disappear with no explanation," she says with a shrug. "I met a hot French guy, anyway."

I nod, relieved. I should have known Molly would have moved on. This is the girl who cheated on her high school boyfriend with his best friend. Twice.

"You still with Mr. Australia?" she asks.

I feel a jab in my heart at the mention of Alexander. I shake my head.

"Since when?" she asks, interested.

"Recently."

I can see in her eyes that she's digesting this information. "Explains why I saw him kissing some blonde two days ago. Guess it didn't take him long to move on. They were really going at it."

Her words hit me like a speeding fist. I'm stunned, but I swallow hard and try not to react.

"That's news to you?" she says, making no effort to hide the schadenfreude behind her eyes. "I hate to say it, but if he's with a new girl that fast it probably means he was cheating on you all along."

I'll never understand why people say "I hate to say it" right before they say something they obviously relish imparting. My heart is still doing a slow freefall through my body when Charlie runs into the foyer and sees me.

"Declan!" he yells out as he barrels over to give me a hug. I kneel down to catch him and he nearly bowls me over.

"Hey big guy, I'm so happy to see you," I say and I mean it even more dearly than usual as I hug him tight, trying to forget Molly's words.

"Declan, you're here!" I peer up to where the voice is coming from and see Mrs. Bing descending the curved staircase. She's dressed to kill in expensive heels and a body-hugging dress. "How nice that you and Molly get a chance to catch up. She just arrived back a few days ago."

Molly mimics gagging and sticking her finger down her throat as she walks away.

"Could you make Charlie dinner?" Mrs. Bing asks as she reaches the bottom of the stairs. "You can pull something together from what's in the fridge. I should be home after midnight. I'll text you if I'm running late." As Mrs. Bing runs through the rest of the instructions for me, I'm hardly listening and her words start to meld together into meaningless *mwah mwah mwah* sounds like the adults in Peanuts cartoons. All I can think about is Alexander kissing someone. *Here.* In San Mar. Mrs. Bing said Molly got back a few days ago so it had to be here … but I thought he was supposed to be halfway around the world? Why didn't he contact me? None of my tormented thoughts get very far because I can't stop the image playing in my mind of him kissing someone else over and over. I feel sick to my stomach. I want to chase after Molly and grill her for details but I won't give her the satisfaction.

Maybe she's lying?

I grasp at that straw with everything I've got.

Chapter Twenty-Four

I haven't tried to contact Alexander since he left. We promised we wouldn't unless it was an emergency but now I can't help myself. I want to call him, right now, and demand to know what's going on. But will his phone even work where he is?

It sure as hell will work if he's here in San Mar, rather than halfway around the world.

Dark, angry thoughts waft over me. How could he do this? Did he lie about where he was going? Does he consider himself free to date other people? As if we're broken up for real? Maybe that's why he told me I should consider myself free …

As I wrestle with the possibilities, puzzle pieces snap into place in my mind. Alenna supposedly left two days ago. Alexander was here, kissing some blonde, two days ago. The words "they were really going at it" play over and over in my mind like a chisel scraping a groove into my heart. Could it have been her? What other blonde would he be with? Are they back together? Would Alenna do that to me? Would Alexander?

He said not to communicate while he's gone but I don't care. I need to talk to him, *right now*, damn any consequences.

I yank out my phone and pull up his number, I'm going to—

"Declan? I'm hungry. Can I eat now?" asks Charlie, breaking through my fury.

I look over at him and take a deep breath. I'm babysitting. I left Charlie in front of the TV. I can't pace around going nuclear when I should be focusing on him and giving him the attention he craves. Not to mention food. When I look at his innocent little face tilted up to me right now asking for dinner it makes me want to hug him tight and protect him from all the hurt in the world.

I take another deep breath and realize I need time to think this through first, anyway. Why is my first instinct to believe Molly and not trust Alexander? I'm feeling blindsided.

I set the phone down.

"Sure, sweetie," I say as I take Charlie's hand and we walk into the kitchen and open the refrigerator. My heart sinks when I see the contents. It's barren, save for about twelve *Be Thin!* protein shakes and a plastic container of celery sticks. Inside the crisper there's a yellow onion, a head of broccoli, and a bag of romaine with a "use by" date of two weeks ago. I look in the pantry for some soup or something edible I can turn into a meal for Charlie but all I find is a box of Cheerios, a can of mushrooms, and a loaf of bread with its best days behind it. I give up. Maybe I should order a pizza.

"You want pizza?" I ask Charlie as he hugs my leg. I fight back revulsion at the mere suggestion after the pepperoni pizza and Slurpee fiasco but I'm feeling desperate and they deliver. We could order a veggie special and drink water.

"Had that for lunch," Charlie says, looking up at me.

"Chinese food?" I ask.

He cocks his head to the side. "Is that the one with the noodles?"

"It can be."

"I had that tomorrow," he says.

"You mean you're going to have it?"

"What's the day that already happened?" he asks, peering up into my eyes.

I smile. "Yesterday."

"I had that yesterday," he says.

I sigh and open the refrigerator again. There's a carton of eggs I didn't notice the first time.

"How about an omelet?" I ask Charlie.

"No."

"Do you know what an omelet is?"

"No," he says again.

"You'll like it," I say. "I know you will."

"How do you know?" he asks.

"Because of the way we'll make it, with fungus and trees in it," I say.

He looks intrigued.

"And worms," I add, drawing out the word to make them sound especially dangerous.

His eyes go wide and his jaw drops open. "Really?" he asks with delight. "Molly will *never* eat that!"

I laugh. "No, I bet she won't," I say. "But we will. We'll love it. Help me make it and you'll see."

We rinse and cut the broccoli "trees" and I show him how the long, curvy onion slices turn into "worms" as we sauté them in a pan with some olive oil. We add the mushroom "fungus" and finally the eggs. We top it off with some "bugs and dirt" (salt and pepper) and Charlie eats it up, literally and figuratively. The best thing is, I managed to distract myself for almost an hour from what's eating me up inside. After we finish, before I can begin to stew over Alexander again, Charlie asks to play some games and that's what we do, non-stop, until it's time for bed when I read him stories until I nearly drift into sleep before he does. I'm exhausted, both physically and mentally.

It's late when Mrs. Bing returns and after she pays me I sit in my mom's car for a long time, pondering what to do. I need to talk to Alexander. I'm tied up in knots and I won't be able to sleep unless I do.

Screw this stupid plan, I'm getting some answers.

Chapter Twenty-Five

I pull up to Alexander's house and sit for a few minutes in the car, wavering. It's late. I can't just go knock on the door and wake up Edwin. He's old. He's probably been asleep for hours. But are old guardians like old people? Or are they young inside?

Who knows? Why am I even thinking about this? All I know is, I need some answers and I've abided by this plan long enough. With my mind resolved, I get out of the car and walk up to the front door, but before I can press the doorbell the door opens.

"Edwin?" I say, startled, as he stands before me in a tailored robe and slippers.

"Come in, Declan," he says, a little resignedly. I glance behind me to see if anyone's watching us as he stands aside to let me in.

"How did you know I was here?" I ask as he leads me to sit down in the kitchen.

"I was reading," he says. "I felt your angst when you drove up."

I'm a little taken aback. I'm so upset he sensed it through the walls?

"I can feel that you want to talk to me about something," he says.

I nod. "I do," I say, as all the stress I've been holding in floods over me like a waterfall, causing my eyes to well up. "But I'm sorry to come here so late."

Edwin takes a deep breath and places his hands over mine on the table. "I know all this worry is taking a toll on you," he says. The understanding and kindness in his expression make me want to cry even more. "But the plan is working," he adds.

"It is?" I ask, meeting his eyes.

"Yes. Avestan left yesterday."

I absorb this information. I'm surprised and not sure how to react. Then I remind myself what drove me here. "Edwin, did Alexander break up with me for real?" I ask.

"Is that what he said?"

"No, not in so many words. But he left it … ambiguous."

Edwin nods. "Consider it part of the plan."

"Was it also part of the plan that he was here in San Mar two days ago?" I ask. "And he didn't even tell me? Or try to see me?" My words spill out in a pain-filled rush.

Edwin meets my eyes, looking sad but understanding. "Yes."

"What about kissing some blonde?" I ask, my eyes welling up. "Was that part of the plan, too?"

I detect a micro-flash of surprise in his eyes. "Where did you hear that?" he asks.

"Molly Bing saw him."

Edwin remains still, pensive. After a stretch of quiet he answers. "Part of the plan."

"Was it Alenna? The girl that he was kissing?"

Edwin meets my eyes. "Declan, I know this is hard—"

"I need to talk to him, Edwin. Please. I need him to call me—"

He shakes his head. "Now would be the worst time to reach out, Declan. Avestan just left. The plan is working. And Alexander can't be distracted. I know you wouldn't want that."

I don't answer. No, I don't want to distract him. Defeating Avestan is the only chance we have to be together. But my heart is breaking inside with all this uncertainty. "But I need some reassurance, Edwin," I implore, "that he hasn't forgotten me." My voice cracks as I say the words.

Edwin cradles both my hands in his. "Declan," he says, "I'll admit I don't know about the kiss. But I do know that Alexander could never forget you. He loves you too much, dear."

I peer up and meet his eyes. Their depths are so kind, and truthful.

"Can you ask Alenna about it?" I ask.

"She isn't here."

Because she's with Alexander.

"Do you trust Alexander?" Edwin asks quietly.

"Yes," I whisper.

"Then trust that he loves you … and that everything he's doing is part of his plan to come back to you. After he's done what he needs to do."

I nod and tears spill down my cheeks. He's right, I do trust Alexander. I know how much he loves me. I just need to remind myself of that. No matter what Queen B said she saw. I stand up from the table and walk over to Edwin and hug him. I know he's not always terribly effusive but he hugs me back, holding me tightly. "Now, now," he says, patting my back, "are you feeling better?"

"Sort of," I say as I wipe away the remnants of wet tears. "How long do you think it will be until Alexander comes back?"

"As long as it takes," Edwin replies. When he sees my expression he adds, "Give it another week, at least, and then we can talk again."

My heart leaps in my chest. *It might only be another week?* I hug him again with a tear-stained smile on my face. "Okay," I say. "I can do that. Thanks, Edwin."

He walks me to the door and watches as I get into my mom's car. After I start the engine I turn back to wave but I see that he's no longer looking at me. His mouth is set in a firm line, preoccupied, as he closes the door.

Chapter Twenty-Six

I won't lie and say I'm not still brooding over that kiss. I know Edwin was right when he reminded me to trust Alexander, and that's what I'm resolved to do, but it was hard to sleep last night and it's impossible to get it out of my mind. I convinced Liz to go with me on my morning run, even though she detests running. I'm thankful for the distraction of her company, which keeps my wandering thoughts at bay.

"What are you up to the rest of the day?" asks Liz as we near the beach.

"I'm working at the shelter and then I promised I'd help Justin, from work, move. What about you?"

"Finn said he has a surprise planned."

I smile.

"You know what it is?" she asks, looking at me.

I smile wider.

"Tell me," she insists. "We go back and forth planning dates for each other and when it's his turn, half the time his surprises are so sweet and romantic I just want to grab him and kiss him, but the other half of the time we end up at the Jet Propulsion Lab in Palo Alto for a discussion of the Higgs-Boson particle."

I laugh. "He told me about that and I have to tell you, he conjured an analogy involving quantum entanglement and the way he feels about you that was pretty moving actually."

"I know," she says with a smile, "he told me. And the lab visit was actually interesting, I have to admit. I love learning about that stuff, it's just not what I was expecting for a date. He doesn't understand that you can't just spring that shit on someone out of the blue when they're expecting dinner and a movie."

I laugh. "You'll like what he has planned today," I say.

"What is it?"

"Don't you want it to be surprise?"

"Not particularly."

"It's simple, and sweet, and I promise you'll like it." Finn is taking her to the river where we used to hang out as kids, for a picnic.

"All right," she says, "you convinced me. Don't say anymore."

"He actually has a bunch of fun things planned for you guys all summer. I think he looked up 'romantic dates' on the internet and made a spreadsheet, ranked according to both of your interests."

She smiles. Liz has turned into a bit of mush pot under Finn's influence and it's pretty hilarious. "You know," she says, "he drives me nuts half the time but he works so damn hard at being thoughtful ... the fact that it doesn't come natural makes me appreciate it more, you know?"

"He's as earnest as they come," I say with a nod. "And loyal."

She smiles. "And cute."

"You're in love," I say with a laugh.

"I was looking at that picture you gave me," she says with a smile, "and I realized that I probably fell for Finn the first time he ever said, 'I didn't know that. Thank you for telling me,' when I explained to him that when I looked at my watch it meant I was obviously bored out of my skull from hearing him talk about how many pull-ups he can do. He was completely sincere the way he said it, and it kinda broke through my crusty, cynical heart …"

I chuckle. Finn's go-to response whenever we tell him something he wasn't aware of—usually involving a social nicety that isn't readily apparent—has always been *'I didn't know that. Thank you for telling me.'* Like when I explained how far to stand away from someone when you're talking, or the fact that people mention the weather just as a conversation filler, not because they're boring. When Finn says it, he genuinely means it, with no guile or sarcasm. It's disarming. Through the years he's catalogued information about nearly every possible social interaction in the files of his brain and he accesses the appropriate guidelines as needed.

Not to say that Finn isn't sarcastic. He and Liz could win awards for their creative use of sarcasm and dry humor. It's just that when you tell him something he didn't know— something that helps him understand all the baffling ins and outs of interacting with other humans—he's genuinely grateful. When we were little he once told me that every day he felt like he was navigating through a maze in a dark room. He'd say something to someone and they'd react in a way he wasn't expecting and he didn't know why. He felt like he kept hitting walls all day and he could never make it out the other side. Eventually, he confessed, he almost gave up. If people were going to get offended without explanation or just walk away when he tried to play with them, why even bother anymore? Maybe he should just turn back and not even try to make his way through the maze every day. I understood his analogy keenly because it was similar to how I felt about my panic attacks. I never knew how to make them stop or when they might strike or if I'd make it through the day without hitting a wall and having one. Now, whenever I see Finn looking uncomfortable in a crowd or at a party, I picture him as that little boy navigating that dark maze, afraid he's going to say the wrong thing and hit another wall and it tugs on my heart. Over the years his confidence has grown, and by high school everyone started being nicer anyway and cutting everyone a little more slack. I think after the gauntlet of middle school and puberty most kids emerge slightly kinder. It's almost impossible not to. Unless you go the other way, I suppose, and double down—like Molly Bing.

Liz and I reach the ocean and she starts heading down the cliffs to the water. We have the option to run further down the path and take the stairs to the beach but Liz is already scrambling down the terraced rocks and dirt, so I follow.

"So why is Justin moving again?" asks Liz when we reach the edge of the shore and take our shoes off so we can let the waves lap over our feet.

"His lease was up," I say, "so he's moving to a new place with one of his roommates."

"And why does he need your help?" she asks.

"He has some friends helping him with the actual move, but he asked for my help unpacking. To help him get organized."

"Does this mean you're finally getting over Alexander a little?"

"What do you mean?"

"What do I mean? I mean I met Justin when I picked you up from work. The guy is hot—with his blue eyes and blonde hair and that sexy surfer bod. And he seems nice, too. Anyone can see he likes you."

I shake my head. "We're just friends."

She raises an eyebrow. "Uh … trust me, Justin has other things in mind."

I stare at her as if she's crazy. "I don't know where you're getting your information, but you're wrong. Besides, I'm pretty sure he's dating some girl named Ella now. She picked him up three days in a row in a convertible."

"I'm 'getting my information' from my own eyes," she says, "and I don't doubt that he's dating another girl—or many girls—but that doesn't mean he can't like you, too."

"We're *friends*."

"Okay," she says, putting her hands up in mock defeat. "I'm just sayin'…" she adds with a glance and a smile in my direction.

I shake my head and can't help but smile back and we're silent for a moment as we both stare out to the ocean and watch the waves break at our feet.

After a while, Liz peers down and wiggles her sand-encrusted toes. "You're not seriously thinking we run all the way back now, are you?" she says. "With sand stuck to our feet? I'm thinking Uber? With maybe a stop on the way home for breakfast? How's that sound?"

I smile at her and shake my head. "All we have to do is let our feet dry and brush off the sand when we get back up to the road," I say. "Then we can put our socks back on. I do this every day. As long as our shoes don't get wet we're fine."

She looks over at me and sticks out her arm in front of her and opens her hand wide, letting her running shoes drop into the water dramatically. "Oops," she says.

I shake my head. "You *kill* me."

"Guess it's Uber and breakfast after all," she responds with a smile.

"So where's your roommate?" I ask Justin as I unpack books and add them to the bookshelf in the main room of his new apartment. It's a two-bedroom, one-bath in a fourplex, nothing spectacular, but it's neat and tidy and it's in a good location near campus. It makes me excited to someday live on my own like this, maybe with Liz. Or Alexander? The thought makes me smile.

"Dylan? He went to Eleuthera for a couple weeks to surf. I couldn't afford to go. Most of this furniture is his. All I have are a few milk crates and some books."

"These boxes aren't yours?"

"Not most of them. I was hoping we could do the kitchen next. Dylan has bowls and silverware and all that kind of junk." He points to a stack of boxes on the kitchen floor. "I figure if I get the kitchen unpacked—even if nothing else gets done—at least I can kick back tonight on the couch, stream a movie on my iPad, and eat a bowl of Lucky Charms."

"For dinner?"

"It's magically delicious," he says with a leprechaun accent.

I laugh. "It's also magically artificial."

"Yeah, my mom used to say that any cereal that turns your milk a different color should be illegal."

"Smart lady," I say as I open another box of books.

"Yep," he says quietly and I recognize the same faraway look in his eyes that I get when I think about my dad.

I decide to change the subject. "Are you going to see your dad this summer?"

"Yeah. I'll be heading up for a week."

"Is he in California?"

"Yeah, but my dad likes to say they're stateless. He remarried a few years ago and they moved to her hometown near the California/Oregon border. The area was once supposed to be a separate state and there's actually a sign on the highway that says 'Welcome to Jefferson, the 51st State.'"

"Really?"

He nods. "My dad thinks it's funny. I guess they had this whole push to be recognized in 1941 but then Pearl Harbor happened and the war started so it never went anywhere."

I shake my head. "I feel like I should know that since I grew up in California but I've never heard of it," I say with amusement. "Wait … are you making it up?"

"No, I swear. I'm full of useless information."

I smile as I fold up the last box of books and we move into the kitchen. "You should put that on your resume. Justin Wright: full of interesting but useless information."

"Already on there," he says with a smile, "I'm way ahead of you." He opens a box filled with bowls, plates, and silverware and slides it between us. "This is where I need your help the most, by the way. I know there's some sort of system to follow when you set up a kitchen but I have no idea what it is."

I look around the small galley-style kitchen. "You just have to think about how you use things and what's most convenient. Like your coffeemaker will go over there, right? So you want the cupboard with your mugs nearby, and also close to the sink. And these ladles and spatulas and things should go next to the stove because that's where you'll use them. It's not exactly rocket science."

His eyebrow rises. "Did I just detect an insult?" he asks. "From Declan Jane?" He tosses a wadded up piece of packing paper at my head.

It bounces off and I grab one from my box and throw it at him and soon we're in the midst of a giant paper war until the floor and counters are covered in crumpled wads.

"I think we're done here," I say, laughing, as we pause and survey our handiwork.

"I'm ready to call it," he says.

I look around. "As tempting as that is, the organizer in me can't leave it this way."

He smiles. "I can do the rest on my own later. You've already helped unpack a ton. And now that you've taught me the secret system to organizing a kitchen, that apparently I was too stupid to recognize before, I think I'm good to go."

I throw another piece of paper at his head. "C'mon," I say. "If we stop messing around we can get these boxes unpacked and this whole kitchen done and dusted in 30 minutes or less."

He meets my eyes. "You really don't mind?" he says. "All right, but you have to let me treat you to dinner afterwards, as a thank you."

"Thanks, but I've already had my fill of Lucky Charms today."

He laughs. "First of all, I don't share my Lucky Charms with just anyone. And second of all, did you really think I was going to offer you some after the way you dissed them earlier? I'm talking a real restaurant—within my limited student budget, of course—maybe Rico's or Tech Sushi."

His mention of food makes me realize how hungry I am. "I haven't had sushi in a while," I say.

"Great, let's toss all this junk into some cupboards and drawers and get out of here."

I smile and throw one more wadded up piece of paper at him and then we set to unpacking for real.

"So what happened with you and your boyfriend, Alexander?"

Justin asks me this question as we're eating at Tech Sushi, directly after I just stuffed another piece of Dragon Roll in my mouth. I'm in the midst of savoring it with my eyes closed and I'm practically moaning it's so delicious.

"He went back to Australia you said?" he asks.

"Yes," I mumble and nod my head as I finish chewing. "But I'd rather not talk about it."

"Okay." He looks at me for a long while as if he wants to say something more and then decides against it.

"You still dating that girl Ella?" I ask.

"No," he says. "Not anymore."

"Why?"

"She had this annoying habit."

"What?"

"The way she chewed."

"Are you serious?" I can't help but wonder what he's been thinking of my chewing as I've been cramming pieces of Dragon Roll in my mouth.

He nods. "We'd watch a movie and she'd get a bag of Ruffles potato chips and she'd put a whole chip in her mouth, one at a time, and the way she pressed it against her tongue and then chewed, I couldn't focus on anything but the sounds she made."

I set down my chopsticks. "Let me get this straight, you broke up with her because you didn't like the way she ate potato chips?"

"Yep," he says without a trace of regret. "That … and because I caught her in bed with another guy at a party … that was probably a factor, too."

I meet his eyes and see humor covering what looks like genuine hurt. "Really?" I say. "That's terrible. I'm sorry."

He nods and I can tell that, like me, he doesn't want to talk about it.

"What about all those other girls I've seen come by for you?" I ask. "You don't seem like you're hurting in the lady department."

"You mean Mandy and Sarah? That wasn't anything serious … mostly just friends."

I nod.

"You gonna finish your edamame?" he asks.

I slide it over. "It's yours."

"You gonna finish that second roll?"

I place my hand protectively over my San Mar Roll, which I plan to devour next. "Off limits," I say.

He laughs. "My dad used to call me the human garbage disposal. I'll eat all your leftovers if you let me."

The rest of our dinner is filled with easy conversation and as Justin pays the check I realize what a nice distraction this evening has been. A short respite from worrying about Alexander and thinking about that kiss and one more day I can check off the calendar until he comes back.

"Thanks again for your help with the unpacking," Justin says as we walk out of the restaurant.

"You're welcome."

"Seriously, you find out who your true friends are when you ask for help moving."

"Your friends who did the actual heavy lifting are the ones to really thank."

"I'll pay for it when they move, believe me."

I smile. "Well thanks for dinner. I'm sorry I ate it all so there aren't any leftovers for the human garbage disposal."

"Ha," he says with a laugh. "Don't worry, I'll manage any residual hunger later with a bowl of Lucky Charms." He looks around the small parking lot. "Where'd you park?"

"Over on Broadway," I say with a nod of my head in that direction. I drove separately so I could go directly home from the restaurant.

"I'll walk you."

We head down the street and around the corner and I stop when I reach my mom's car.

"What's this?" he asks. "Where's Archie?"

"I thought I told you, Archie's gone. This is my mom's."

His eyes run over my mom's dark grey Chevy Volt. "I guess you don't have to worry about running out of gas anymore," he says. "But what happened?"

"Long story. I ended up having to sell him to a mechanic."

"Geez, really? I'm sorry," he says, sounding genuinely bummed, "that must have been tough, selling your first car. Like losing an old friend."

I look up, surprised at the genuineness of his empathy and how well he understands. Our eyes meet. "Yeah," I say quietly, "it was. Exactly like that."

And that's when it happens.

Justin bends down swiftly and kisses me.

I'm so stunned at first that I freeze. His lips are foreign-feeling, but not unpleasant, and as he kisses me gently I feel myself almost starting to kiss him back before I suddenly come to my senses. In that moment, as our lips part, I sense someone watching from across the street and when I see who it is my stomach falls to my feet.

It can't be.

I'm thrilled, and faint, and sick all at once.

It's Alexander.

Chapter Twenty-Seven

Alexander's eyes lock with mine for an instant and the expression on his face causes my heart to plunge straight into the ground. As I absorb that this is real, not a dream, my brain finally sends the signals for normal operation to the rest of my body, but before I can react Alexander turns and walks away.

Justin is still standing before me, looking hurt and confused. "Justin," I say, my words coming out in a jumble, "I'm sorry … if I gave you the wrong impression I … we're just friends … and I'm sorry but I have to go … right now."

I take off, leaving Justin looking baffled on the sidewalk as I run across the middle of the street and up the other side to the corner where Alexander was standing. Desperately, I look down the street in the direction he was headed but I don't see him. I follow anyway, dodging groups of people who are strolling downtown, and trying to make my way as fast as I can. I stop and scan through the crowds in every direction at the next block but I still don't see him. I go the next block and still no sign. He could have gone anywhere. My heart is pounding in my chest. *What do I do?*

I take out my phone and call his number but it just rings, never picking up. I hang up and try a few more times with the same result. As my heart slows and the reality of what has happened sets in, I feel as though my chest has been cleaved in two. Alexander came back, and he found me this time, only to see me kissing someone else. I go to the next block, and the next, and the next, but I still don't see him. Finally, it sinks in as I search in all directions that I won't find him—he's gone. And he left with the memory of me kissing Justin burned in his mind.

I'm frozen, stunned, and somehow I manage to thaw my limbs and walk slowly back in the direction of the car, wiping away tears and trying not to make eye contact with the people passing in the other direction.

When I reach my mom's car and I slide into the driver's seat, I hear my phone chime in my purse. I slide it out and look at the screen. There's a text from Alexander and when I see his words I want to cry all over again. His message is one short sentence only:

It's better this way.

Chapter Twenty-Eight

I try to call Alexander back but it just rings and rings. I text him but there's no reply. I drive straight to Edwin's house, not knowing what else to do.

"Alexander is here," I say as he lets me in.

"In San Mar?"

"Yes, I just saw him."

"*Damn it,*" he growls, "I told him not to come."

"Why?"

"I shouldn't have, but I asked him about the kiss. He wanted to explain it to you in person. I told him it was too dangerous. I warned him Avestan might see him … and traveling by light and back would sap his energy … I should have known he wouldn't listen. What did he say to you?"

"I didn't talk to him," I say. "That's why I'm here, I—"

"Edwin, Avestan is back. I came to tell you as soon as—" Alenna walks in the kitchen but stops speaking abruptly when she sees me.

The fact that she said Avestan is back doesn't even phase me, I'm so single-mindedly focused on Alexander. "Alenna, you need to help me find Alexander," I say with urgency. "He's here and I saw him but—"

"Alexander came back to explain a kiss to Declan that apparently you and he shared," Edwin says, cutting me off.

Alenna looks surprised. And so am I, frankly. My suspicions were right—it *was* Alenna. She turns to look at me. "Declan, it's not what you think."

"What was it then?" I ask.

"Avestan didn't follow Alexander at first, so we staged the kiss so he would see it."

As Alenna explains, I notice Edwin look at her with an expression that's hard to decipher.

"Why?" I ask.

"Because Avestan loved me once," Alenna says. "We needed to remind him how much he hates Alexander, for having what he could never have … to make him follow Alexander away from San Mar. And we wanted him to think that Alexander and I are back together, so he'll believe the two of you are through."

"I told him not to come back," Edwin says. "That you trusted him and he could explain the full story to you later." He casts another glance at Alenna.

The memory of what occurred tonight rolls over me in a thick wave of nausea. "But he saw me kissing someone," I say, my voice desperate and laced with anguish. "That's why I didn't get to talk to him. He left. Before I could explain."

"You were *kissing* someone?" Alenna asks. I look over at Edwin and the disappointment on his face, too, is like a spear through my heart.

"It wasn't like that," I say, pleading with them to hear me out. "It was a friend from work. He kissed me out of the blue when I wasn't expecting it." The words pour out in a jumble. "I love Alexander. I would never cheat on him. You have to believe me."

Alenna sighs heavily. "I learned long ago not to get caught up in the drama of mortals."

"But that's just it," I insist desperately. "There's no drama. It was a mistake. And I corrected it. I just need to tell Alexander. I need to explain."

Alenna's eyes meet mine and I detect disdain, or doubt, or maybe both. It makes me feel sick inside.

"I need to talk to Alexander," I say again softly. "Can you please tell me if there's any way I can reach him? To explain?" The desperation in my voice is palpable. "He sent me this text, and he won't answer his phone … and I just need to talk to him."

Edwin looks at me. "I'm sure he already left by now," he says quietly. "When I talk with him I'll try to explain, but I don't think we should distract him with any more communications about misunderstood kisses or anything else for now. He needs to focus, gain his strength, and be ready when the time is right."

Alenna nods. "He's killing himself for you, halfway around the world, fighting some monster. The last thing we need is for you to distract him any more than you already have."

As I absorb the pain of Alenna's final jab, I understand that she's only looking out for her friend. She doesn't know me. Not really. She doesn't realize how much I love Alexander. How much I think about him every day and worry, hoping he's okay. How I could never forget him or betray him in any way. She knows mortals, and all of our disappointing fallibilities, and she doesn't want Alexander fighting for something that isn't worth it. I understand why that's her view. But as I play her words over and over in my mind, I realize there's one thing I don't understand. And it's causing my heart to beat faster in my chest.

He's killing himself halfway around the world for you.

Fighting some monster.

But Alenna just said Avestan is here …

So who is Alexander fighting?

Chapter Twenty-Nine

"What monster?" I ask.

Edwin looks at Alenna but neither answer.

"You just said Avestan is here," I say, my voice rising with emotion. "So what monster is Alexander fighting?"

"Alenna, why don't you leave us," Edwin says. "Go check in with the other guardians to make sure Avestan didn't see Alexander when he was here."

Alenna nods and leaves.

"What monster?" I ask again, determined.

"Why don't we sit down," he says, gesturing to chairs around the kitchen table.

"Edwin, you're worrying me," I say as he sits down slowly. "What monster?"

"Has Alexander explained to you the concept of Makers?"

I nod. "They're the ones who turn dark guardians. If you destroy the Maker, you destroy the whole line."

He shakes his head. "Not quite. You can *weaken* the whole line."

"Alexander said destroy," I say.

Edwin nods. "He's correct in that they would be weakened so severely their influence would be minimal. Effectively destroyed. It happens gradually, like a spreading disease throughout the line."

I swallow the lump in my throat. "Is the monster he's fighting Avestan's Maker?"

"Yes," he says grimly.

"But Alexander said he can't be destroyed."

"He can be wounded. And if he can be wounded badly enough, the whole line would suffer a loss of power. Much the same as what Avestan suffered in Nusquam. It could buy you some time again."

"But why would Alexander even try? I thought the whole plan was to fight Avestan? Once and for all? Away from here?"

He nods. "It was, but with Avestan avoiding him and continuing to dither over leaving San Mar, Alexander decided to pursue other avenues. He was hoping it might further entice Avestan to leave so he could defeat him directly, and if not, he hopes to weaken him by wounding his Maker. Either way, Alexander could return sooner."

"Why can't his Maker be destroyed?" I ask.

Edwin shakes his head. "It's not easy to explain."

"Edwin, I need to understand what Alexander is facing."

He pauses for a moment, meeting my eyes, before he answers. "When you think of light energy," he says, "think of it as a natural state. It's the state we're inclined to be in, all things being equal and balanced. It diffuses and spreads naturally. The connection is all around us, like a blanket. You can do something positive that tugs on one corner of the blanket and it can affect another corner, far away."

I nod and he continues.

"Dark energy, on the other hand, requires influence— sometimes only a nudge, other times a hard, sustained force— to push things out of balance. But once it tips, it can become entrenched, and then it's difficult to shift. The connection is more linear, from one to another. A line can be drawn from where it started to all the places it is now, like branches of a growing tree."

I nod. I think I understand well enough.

"Dark and light are inextricably linked," he says, "with a balance that favors light."

"Because light spreads more easily," I say.

He shakes his head. "It's true that the arc of energy, over time, bends toward nobler interests over sinister. But once dark energy tips, it can spread quickly. It's a powerful force."

"How does this relate to Avestan's Maker?"

"If you imagine the tree of dark energy—an ancient tree—Avestan's Maker is close to the beginning."

"So he's part of the trunk rather than the branches."

"More like part of the seed."

I swallow.

"Does he have a name?" I ask.

"Yes," he says gravely. "Malentus. And if Avestan doesn't leave San Mar very soon, so that Alexander can take him on directly, I'm afraid Alexander's plan is to take on Malentus instead."

Chapter Thirty

I leave Edwin's house with my heart in my throat. Why is Alexander risking himself so recklessly? And the thought of him putting his plan at risk by traveling here only to be rewarded by the vision of me kissing Justin makes me feel sick inside all over again. Now he's weaker than before and unless Avestan follows him soon, he's planning to fight Malentus. Someone even worse.

And he's risking it all for me, a girl he now thinks betrayed him.

When I get home, I try to call him again, fruitlessly. I read his message over and over: *It's better this way.* It hurts, physically, to think of how he must have felt when he typed it. If he won't answer his phone, maybe he'll read a text from me. I texted him earlier and asked him to call but he didn't respond. I know Edwin said I shouldn't distract him ... but I mull it over and decide that it's more important for Alexander to hear an explanation. Otherwise he'll be wondering how I could betray him so cruelly.

I start typing several times and then delete it all and start over. Finally I settle on short, simple sentences.

> Remember when Molly kissed you? That's what this was. I wasn't expecting it. Justin is just a friend. I stopped it.

I wait for a response but don't see the typing indicator pop up.

I decide to keep sending more texts, hoping he has his phone and he'll see and read them all.

> Please believe me
> I love you
> I miss you
> I'm so sorry.

I wait, but still no response so I text again.

> Please at least give me a
> sign that you received
> this

I stare at the screen for long minutes with teary eyes and still don't get a reply. I send a final message.

> I'll wait for you forever

I set the phone down as tears escape, falling down my face and clouding my vision. Several more minutes go by without a response and I wipe away tears and type one last request. The most important.

> Please Alexander, please
> don't go after Malentus.

I press send and wipe away more tears and wait expectantly. Nothing.

I decide to take a shower to try to forget my misery for a while, but as I start to strip off my clothes, I have a thought. I sit down at my desk. I remember Alexander once telling me that one of the reasons he likes being out in the ocean is because it's quiet. It's away from mortals and the cacophony of endless emotions they exude and it's a chance to be peaceful in nature. He said that when he's out on the water he can recharge and communicate more clearly with all of the energy in the universe.

If he can't, or won't, read my texts, maybe I can communicate with him another way.

I open the top drawer of my desk and pull out a piece of stationery. Then I pick up a pen and pour out what's in my heart.

Dear Alexander,

The thought that you finally came back and saw me kissing someone else weighs so heavily on me that I can hardly write these words. Justin is only a friend, nothing more, and I could go on and on to explain the mistake, but I saw the look on your face. I understand if you're not ready to listen. But please, if by some miracle you get this, please read it anyway, all the way through.

Alexander, I miss you, every minute of every day, and I love you with all my heart. I fear for you with Avestan, and, even more so now that Edwin told me about Malentus. Please, Alexander, don't do it. Don't go after someone so evil. Edwin says it's a battle that can't be won. He and Alenna are protecting me from Avestan. You don't need to risk your life. There must be another way to end this.

Please understand that for me it's not "better this way," as you said in your message. The only thing that could ever be better for me is to know you're safe from harm. I don't think I could live in a universe where you no longer exist. Even if you don't come back to me ... which I desperately hope you do.

Please be safe, Alexander. If you can somehow feel all the love in my heart you'll know I'm telling the truth.

I love you. Always.

Declan

I fold up the letter with tears in my eyes, stuff it in my pocket and go downstairs and into the garage, where I search through boxes until I find what I'm looking for. Then I get on my bike and ride to the ocean.

Chapter Thirty-One

When I get to the cliffs I park my bike and walk down to the water. In my hand is one of the leftover sky lanterns we launched after graduation during a bonfire celebration on the beach. The same sky lanterns my mom and I used to send off to my dad. At the water's edge I tuck my letter under the inside of the lantern frame and light the fuel cell with a match. The paraffin wax flames to life, turning the paper lantern into a glowing, golden lamp and as I let go of the frame so it can rise up into the sky, I whisper Alexander's name. The luminous orb is hauntingly beautiful as it floats silently up and ever higher and out over the sea. I stare after it, watching the light get smaller and smaller as it soars aloft in the sky until finally the light grows dim and appears to flicker and go out, or perhaps it's just so far away now that I can't see it anymore.

Please Alexander, please get this message.

I walk back up the cliffs with tears in my eyes and get back on my bike. I notice a lone man standing on the other side of the road near the streetlight, watching me, but whereas normally I'd wonder and worry if it was another dark guardian, I can't bring myself to care anymore.

I turn my bike in the other direction and ride home.

I wake in the morning exhausted. I check my phone and am dejected to find no messages. I get up to go to the bathroom but I don't even try telling my sorry, swollen-eyed reflection in the bathroom mirror that I should go for my run. The whole

Fallen

"you'll thank yourself later" routine is not going to work. Not today. I drag myself back to bed.

A few minutes later I hear the ding of an incoming text and my heart leaps in my chest. *Maybe it's Alexander.* I immediately grab my phone from the nightstand but when I peer at the screen I almost feel guilty for how disappointed I am. It's a message from Finn.

> Can we practice
> driving now?

Is he serious? It's seven in the morning. I type a reply.

> It's a little early.

He replies quickly.

> My driving test is
> today at 2:30.

> What??? You signed
> up for the test already?

I see the typing indicator bubble pop up and then his reply appears.

The last time you took me driving you said I'd be ready for my test "soon." So I went online and chose soonest available.

I groan. I'm not sure if Finn's quite ready yet. But he's obviously excited—it took him a long time to gain confidence in his driving and the last thing I want to do is set him back. He's so afraid of causing an accident he insists on going at precisely whatever speed limit is posted, except in the case of inclement weather (a question that was on the test for his driver's permit), in which case he goes at a speed "safe for current conditions." I finally convinced him he could go within five miles over the limit on the freeway. I think he memorized the entire California vehicle code. He'll be the safest freakin' driver in the state.

I take a deep breath, trying to summon any amount of nascent energy, before I type out my reply.

K. I'll be there in 30.

I slowly get up off the bed and go back into the bathroom to splash water on my face. I look in the mirror and consider telling him to reschedule the test and then I shake my head. I'm probably being too cautious, he'll do fine. He's by-the-book, exactly what those DMV testing people probably like. I just wanted to be a thousand percent sure he'd pass the first time because he beats himself up so much when he fails.

I grab a granola bar in the kitchen and guzzle down some water before I leave. My mom is still sleeping.

When I turn my bike onto his street it's obvious something's wrong right away. There's a car parked askew in the middle of the street in front of Finn's house and I can see Finn in his jeans kneeling in front of the car. My heart is in my throat and as I get closer and see why Finn's kneeling in the street, tears spring to my eyes and I swallow a sob. Finn is crying silently and petting Zeno, our sweet, gentle soul of a dog. Only Zeno's not moving. He's lying on the ground and his eyes are closed and he's whimpering softly in obvious pain.

"I'm sorry, I'm sorry," cries the girl standing behind us, next to her car. Her face is anguished and tears are spilling down her face. "He just ran out! I didn't see him."

None of this makes sense. Zeno never runs out in the road or chases cars. All he ever wants to do is sit under his tree or lie on the couch next to Finn, or between Finn and me both when I visit. How did he even get out from the back yard?

Yet none of those questions matter because here he is, lying in the middle of the street, and Finn's crying over him and my heart is broken and I don't know what to do. Finn's dad emerges from the house, walking quickly, his phone to his ear, asking questions, and I can tell he's talking to the emergency pet hospital. Mrs. Cooper comes out and puts her hands over her mouth and bursts into tears. Mr. Cooper bends down to check Zeno's injuries while he's on the phone and then he and Finn gently lift him and carry him to the front yard, laying him on the grass. "Go get the car," Mr. Cooper says to Mrs. Cooper and she nods and goes quickly inside to get her keys. Mr. Cooper stays on the phone with the vet and he walks over to talk to the girl who hit Zeno. She's still standing in the street looking stricken.

Finn and I are left alone with Zeno and I kneel down and we pet him gently, trying to soothe him as we listen to his labored breathing and soft whimpers. "It's okay, Zeno," I say softly through tears, "hang in there. Please, Zeno, hang in there, buddy."

"You'll be okay, boy," Finn says to him quietly with tears in his eyes. Then he turns to me. "Will you stay with Zeno while I go in and get him a blanket?" he asks, his voice is strained and the depth of sadness in his eyes is fathomless.

I nod. "Of course."

I stay with Zeno, silently praying that I'll wake up any moment and this will all be just a nightmare. My heart aches so keenly I can barely breathe. As I sit with my hand on Zeno's side, listening with agony to his labored breathing and encouraging him to hang in there, a cold, black shudder runs over me and I feel compelled to look up.

There in the distance, standing on the corner, is Avestan. Watching.

A slow, sickening smile forms on his face and he raises his hand in a wave. As my eyes register horror at what he's done, he turns and walks away.

Chapter Thirty-Two

I want to run after him. I want to *kill him* with my bare hands. I don't care what powers Avestan has, I'll murder him right now for hurting Zeno or I'll die trying. My heart is thrashing in my chest and I'm consumed with anger but I can't leave Zeno here in the grass alone. I look around to see if Finn has come back yet and that's when I feel a hand on my shoulder.

I turn and let out a rush of relief when I see that it's Edwin.

"Avestan did this," I spit out in anguish, tears falling freely. "I just saw him on the corner. You have to do something Edwin, now, please. *Please.*"

Edwin looks around and kneels beside me. He places his palms on Zeno's side and I immediately feel Zeno's body heat. His eyes close and the whimpering stops and I see shimmering light under Edwin's hands as he runs them over Zeno's body from head to tail and down each leg to his paws. I peer over my shoulder and see that Mr. Cooper is walking towards us, and the girl and the car blocking the street are now gone. Edwin quickly removes his hands from Zeno and meets my eyes with a hopeful look.

Relief floods over me and I take his hand and squeeze it, tears overflowing. "Thank you, Edwin," I whisper. "*Thank you.*"

I look up to see Mrs. Cooper scurrying out of the house with her purse on her shoulder and keys in her hand with Finn close behind holding a blanket. When they reach us, Zeno's eyes are now half open and he's breathing evenly. Edwin helps Mr. Cooper load Zeno into the car and Finn lays the blanket over him and stays with him in the back seat while Mr. and

Mrs. Cooper climb in the front. Mrs. Cooper turns to me, bereft and frantic, "I left eggs cooking on the stove, Declan," she says. "Can you turn it off?"

"Yes, of course," I say. "Call me, please, to let me know what the vet says," I say to them as they start to back out of the driveway. Finn nods, looking so worried it makes my heart ache.

As we watch them disappear around the corner all I can think about is that I can't keep putting all the people I love in danger. This has to stop.

Chapter Thirty-Three

I follow Edwin to his house after we leave Finn's. I sit down in the kitchen and Edwin heats some water on the stove for tea.

"How did you know to come?" I ask.

"A guardian alerted me," he says gravely.

"Avestan did this to hurt me," I say with emotion.

Edwin takes my hand. "Yes," he says. "He did it to hurt you deeply. As it has." He meets my eyes with tender compassion. "I'm so sorry, Declan. He's retaliating for what happened in Nusquam in a way I didn't see coming. You humiliated him and he's lashing out simply to hurt with no other gain. This was my failure. Avestan knows that if he causes pain to those around you, the hurt is greater than if he attacked you directly. I was protecting Finn and his family. I didn't realize he would also target Zeno."

I shake my head. "If it weren't for your protection he might have hurt Finn," I say and the thought sends fresh tears to my eyes.

Edwin looks up at me. "I don't know how you'll feel about this but I don't think we should tell Alexander."

"Because he'd want to come back," I say, finishing Edwin's thought.

"Yes, and because Avestan might be treating this as a test."

"How?" I ask.

"He may want to see if it makes Alexander come back."

I take a moment to consider his words. "This is all a game to him?" My voice is filled with contempt. "Hurting children? Hurting innocent animals? Trying to move a game piece here, and see if another piece moves over there? It's sick! And evil."

Edwin nods. "Yes, it is. But if Alexander doesn't come back, Avestan may finally realize the only way to fight him is to follow him, away from here."

I feel so angry inside and I can barely contain it. "Can't we just go find Avestan right now and destroy him?" I ask. "If we all work together—"

"It wouldn't work," Edwin says.

"Why?"

"He won't engage with anyone else to that level until he destroys Alexander," he says. "He's obsessed and he'll do anything, to the point of putting himself at risk, to make it happen. His hate is his greatest power and also his greatest liability. It drives him, just as Alexander's love for you drives him to the same risks."

I'm taken aback by his answer. Alexander is risking his life for me. Zeno nearly died because of me. Little Charlie Bing was placed in mortal danger, also because of me.

For the first time I almost wish we could sail back in time to before Alexander and I met, only this time he could leave me at the mercy of my panic attacks and let Avestan do his worst.

At least then I'd be the only one hurt.

Chapter Thirty-Four

Why doesn't Alexander send me a sign? Anything? Finn called from the pet hospital to say Zeno's going to be okay and the relief in his voice and the relief I felt hearing the news made me burst into tears. I can't stop thinking about how much I want to find Avestan and kill him, with my bare hands, for what he did. I take a shower and remind myself over and over that Zeno is okay, as I let the water pour over me, but I can't let it go. Why can't Avestan just leave us all alone and let me be with Alexander and stop hurting everyone around me? I'm sick to my stomach again when I think about Alexander and whether or not he's fighting Malentus. Or Avestan. Take your pick. He's putting himself in so much danger from all sides. When I get out of the shower it's still only 9:30 a.m. and I don't have to be to Fields and Morris until noon. I think I'll go mad if I can't stop all these thoughts and the worry coursing through me like venom.

I survey my room as I get dressed. The closet and drawers are overflowing. I start tossing all my clothes furiously into a big heap on my bed and then I quickly separate them into categories: keep, donate, and attic storage. In the mood I'm in, I'm probably getting rid of too much but I'm obsessed with the task because it's distracting me from all of my overwhelming emotions. When I can finally open and close my dresser drawers freely without having to shove down clothes, it actually feels good. And satisfying. And I realize how foreign that seems. I haven't felt good in a while.

I place the plastic lid on a storage bin for the attic and I pull down the folding attic stairs from the ceiling in the hallway. Willow, my cat, trots in from my father's old office where she's been taking a nap to see what's going on. "You coming with me into the attic?" I ask and she meows back as if she understands. Willow "talks" to you in cat-speak that honestly sounds more like words than meows. One time, right before she threw up in the hallway, I swear she looked at me and said "*Mama?*" Her vocalizations are eerily clear and I think she was asking me why the heck she was sick. When I was seven I made a wish on my birthday for Willow to be able to speak and I kind of feel like it came true. I pick up the bin and trudge up the attic steps one at a time. Willow follows behind me. At the top of the stairs I flick the light switch on, illuminating the cavernous space. Bins of holiday decorations and other household detritus are neatly labeled and stacked on shelves lining one wall. I move some bins to make room for the container I'm adding and as I shift things around Willow jumps up onto the shelf in the empty space. "C'mon, Willow, I need that spot," I say as I move some boxes she disappeared behind so I can find her and lift her down. When I spot her, she's sitting on top of a plastic file box that was shoved to the back of the shelf. It isn't labeled, which is very unlike my mom. I slide it out and Willow hops off and rubs against my shin, purring. I lift off the lid and look inside.

The first file folder holds a big stack of printouts of what look like spreadsheets. I skim the rest of the folders and see that they hold copies of Fields and Morris legal documents. This must have been my dad's. A wave of melancholy rolls through me as I picture him flipping through these folders as I am now, working at home. I look more closely at the documents and the name on one of the file folders catches my eye. It's the estate for Esther Winchester. The same file that went missing the day that I drove to the courthouse and Archie's engine went out driving back. I forgot to ask Justin about that. I decide to close up the box and when I start to lift it I feel something heavy shift within. I take the lid off once more and push the file folders back to reveal a 5"x7" black leather hardbound book lying on the bottom of the box. I open it to see a hand-written ledger of some sort with amounts and dates and initials marking each entry. I flip through all the pages and on the last page of entries there's a post-it note in my father's handwriting that says simply, "Marty?"

Marty. Maybe Martin Morris, the other law partner at the firm? Mr. Morris retired just after my father died.

I grab a stick-on label and a black sharpie from a Ziploc bag hanging from the shelves and write "Declan's room stuff" on the label and slap it onto my bin. I consider putting my dad's file box back on the shelf, too, but I decide I want to look at it some more. "C'mon, Willow," I say and she follows me down the stairs. When we get back to my room I place the box on the floor of my now-spacious closet and Willow hops on top and sits down. I take a few moments to admire my handiwork. At least now my surroundings have breathing space, even if I'm still an anxious mess inside.

My phone rings and I follow the sound of the ringtone and manage to locate it on the floor under the large garbage bag marked "Donate." It's Liz.

"Hey," I say, answering.

"You, me and Finn are watching movies," Liz declares. "With Zeno. On the couch. All day. Finn just got home and he needs a distraction while Zeno recuperates."

I love how she just announces things, as if it's a fait accompli.

"Be here in ten minutes," she adds.

"I can't," I say, "I have to work at noon."

She groans. "All right, we'll see you tonight then."

"What are you watching?"

"I don't know the name of it … Finn?" she calls out, not bothering to shield the phone from her mouth, "what's the name of this movie again?"

I hear a faint voice in the background. "What?" Liz says again, loudly.

"He's in the other room changing his shirt," she says, "I can't understand him." Then her voice lowers to almost a whisper. "I don't even care what movie it is, I just want to take his mind off what almost happened. Zeno's sitting next to me on the couch now, napping."

"How's he doing?" I ask. "Finn called from the vet and he said he was going to be okay."

"Yeah," she says. "The vet couldn't believe it. No major injuries. It's like he had a guardian angel looking out for him or something. It's a miracle."

My eyes well up again at the memory of him whimpering in pain until Edwin healed him with his hands. "Yeah," I say, "it is."

I stuff my purse and a jacket into my backpack and throw in a couple granola bars and a bottled water. My mom's out today showing houses again so I plan to ride my bike to work. As I'm getting ready to leave I hear the doorbell.

I peek out the peephole before opening the door. It's a kindly-looking man in a blue uniform holding a package.

"Declan Jane?" he says when I open the door.

"Yes."

"This is for you," he says with a smile. He hands me a small brown package and walks away.

I call out thank you and he raises his hand in a wave of acknowledgement and I close the door. *What's this?* I turn it over and note that there's no return address and, in fact, no address for me either. Just my name, printed neatly, on the front. I pull open the door again and look around outside for the man but now he's gone. I don't recall having seen a delivery truck. Maybe he was a private courier.

My heart begins to pound. What if it's from Avestan? But the delivery man smiled so nicely … if he was a dark guardian would he do that? A sickening feeling hits my stomach as I remember Avestan's smile after Zeno was hit.

Please let it be from Alexander.

Chapter Thirty-Five

The package is flat and rectangular and my hands are shaking as I tear the paper. I pause for a second, hesitating. Then, with my heart beating a ferocious rhythm of curiosity mixed with trepidation, I tear the rest of the paper off.

Under the plain brown paper is a sealed cardboard box, and when I maneuver my fingers under the seam to tear it open I find a smaller rectangular box, wrapped in beautifully fine silver wrapping paper, and tied with an exquisite cobalt blue ribbon. I slide off the ribbon and gently ease the silver paper open with my fingers where the ends meet, trying not to tear it. Surely something this beautiful can't be from Avestan.

Inside is a picture frame with a notecard. I turn the frame over, so nervous I can hear my blood rushing in my ears, and when I see the photo inside, my heart swells and tears come to my eyes.

It's a picture of a heart and initials carved into a large, beautifully-weathered tree stump with bright beams of sun shining down in the background like a beacon from the sky. Inside the heart it says: "A.R. loves D.J. Always"

I open the card and wipe my tears with the back of my hand so I can read the handwriting inside:

Dearest Declan,

Please forget about the kiss. I have. I'm not surprised someone else wanted to kiss you. I'd kiss you every minute of every day if I could.

I admit I was hurt at first, and I can't help thinking you'd be better off with a mortal, but upon reflection and a discussion with Edwin, I realize that you had every right. I left, and I told you to consider yourself free. Not to mention the fact that you heard about my kiss with Alenna, with no context to explain.

I'm still waiting for Avestan. He can't hold out much longer—his desire for revenge is too great not to follow me here. In the meantime, I'm doing good work in this corner of the world but it's a never-ending struggle. As for Malentus, as I always say (and I imagine you're shaking your head as you read this), I have a plan ... if I need it. I have to put an end to this, one way or another, once and for all, so you can be safe.

There aren't any redwoods where I am, but I found what remains of this old tree in a peaceful clearing and I come here often to think of you. I feel your energy reaching me through the rays of sunlight that shine through the trees in the afternoon and it makes me smile. I carved our initials here to match what we wrote in the fairy ring in Redwood Park, but with one difference. Your present to me was "D.J. loves A.R. Always." My present to you is my reply. It comes from the heart, just as yours did.

I think about you every day, Declan. I won't be able to communicate again for a while but think about me at midnight tonight, your time. I'm going to send some energy your way and I hope you feel it.

Please know that I love you, babe.

Always,

Alexander

Tears of happiness dribble onto the card and my heart lifts in a way I didn't think possible with Alexander still gone. *Did he get my letter?*

It's not clear, perhaps he only talked with Edwin, but he understands what happened and, best of all, he loves me still and he's *coming back to me*.

My heart is soaring inside.

Short of having Alexander home, this is the best gift I could ever imagine.

Chapter Thirty-Six

Justin looks up at me when I walk into the conference room at Fields and Morris. This is the first time we've seen each other since our kiss debacle. "Hi," I say as normally as I can.

He looks guilty. Or uncomfortable. Or both. "Declan," he says, "listen, I'm sorry about last night. We were having such a good time—at least I thought we were, and—"

"We were," I say. "And it's okay. I'm sorry if I gave you the wrong impression. But I can only be friends. I know I told you I broke up with Alexander but—"

"Enough said," he says, putting up his hand to cut me off. "I misread the situation."

He looks wounded and I feel terrible. First Ella cheats on him and now I'm rejecting him, too. I nod and a long stretch of silence follows.

"The thing is, though," he says, finally breaking the silence, "I'm pretty sure our friendship is doomed now ... to painful awkwardness, or awkward painfulness, or one of those anyway."

"I don't think so—"

"Trust me," he says, "it is. Unless we can somehow forget that the whole kiss thing ever happened." He looks at me with a combination of direful and hopeful eyes.

"Not a chance," I say after a brief moment of considering how best to reply. "The way you came at me like a thief in the night? I don't think I can ever let you live that down."

His blue eyes flash utter surprise for a split second and then he laughs out loud. "You're back to your insults. Now I know we're good."

I smile back, relieved the gambit worked. "I'm sorry I ran off," I say. "That must have seemed awfully weird."

"No more weird than me coming at you like a thief in the night."

I laugh, relieved I don't have to explain.

"Thanks again, by the way, for throwing wads of packing paper all over my kitchen," he says.

"All in a day's work," I chuckle. I sit down at my computer, happy we're back to normal, and get ready to start scanning.

The door to the conference room opens and we both look up. "Declan," Mr. Fields says when he sees me. "You're here. I have a question about some files you scanned."

"Yes?" I answer.

"You put a flag on some old files in the database," he says. "The Winchester estate … why is it flagged?"

"Oh, that," I say, remembering. "I started scanning a box with the Winchester files in it and then I had to deliver some documents to the court in San Jose—that day that you asked me to—and when I got back the box was gone. I flagged it to remind me to look for it because it isn't complete."

"Oh," he says, nodding. "Forget about it. Take the flag off. Unimportant."

I nod. "Sure, okay."

"When you flag things," he explains with a smile, "they show as urgent, and that case closed out a long time ago."

"Okay," I say, "no problem. By the way, I think I may have found those files you were asking for, of my dad's. They were in the attic. One of them was related to the Winchester estate. Do you still want me to bring them in?"

He looks surprised. "Yes," he says, "that would be helpful."

After Mr. Fields leaves I turn to Justin. "I've been meaning to ask you. Did you move that box I was scanning that day? It was the day you left early to pack for your move."

He shakes his head. "Have no idea what you're talking about. I don't mess with your work area. You've got some system going on over there and I'm afraid if I touch anything I'll knock a paper out of 90 degree alignment and the whole thing will blow to hell."

"Very funny," I say, tossing a wad of paper at his head. "I didn't see you mocking my organizational skills when I planned your kitchen for maximum efficiency."

"Was that before or after you threw paper wads everywhere?" he asks. "Like you're doing now."

I crumple up another piece of paper and toss it at him and he chuckles and then we settle in to get back to work.

Soon after I hear my phone chime and I pick it up to see a text from Alenna.

> I'll pick u up today.
> For safety. U off at 5?

What a strange message. I tap out my reply and press send.

> Yes. I get off at 5.
> What do you mean for safety?
> Is something wrong?

The typing indicator bubble pops up and then I see her response.

> Just being cautious.
> See u out front.

I go out to the parking lot at five o'clock and I see Alenna standing by her Mercedes. I unlock my bike and wheel it over. "Will this fit?" I say.

She nods. "Let's get it in the trunk."

She opens the trunk and we lift it and I see her looking past me, over my shoulder.

"Is that the guy that kissed you? Justin?" she asks.

I turn to see Justin walking across the parking lot towards us, with Mr. Fields.

"Yes," I say with a nod. "He's a nice guy. He just misread my intentions."

She meets my eyes. "For what it's worth, I'm not mad at you, Declan. Like I said, I don't get involved in mortal drama. My main priority is protecting you and that's what I'm focused on. I know you love Alexander ... and he loves you. That's very clear."

"Thanks, Alenna," I say, glad we're back on semi-normal terms.

Justin and Mr. Fields reach us. "I was just telling Justin here that I had a client cancel last minute on a whale watching tour I had planned," says Mr. Fields. "I asked around the office and most everyone is busy so I wanted to know if you and Justin would like to join me? Your friend here can come, too," he says, nodding to Alenna. "If you've never been whale watching, it's amazing to see."

Alenna looks at me and shrugs. "You up for it?" she asks.

"This is my friend Alenna, by the way," I say to Mr. Fields and Justin. "Alenna, this is Mr. Fields, my boss, and Justin, my co-worker."

Alenna nods and they all shake hands.

"What do you think," Mr. Fields asks again, "do you want to go?"

"Sure," I say, looking over at Alenna who's nodding her head in agreement. "Thanks, Mr. Fields."

"Great," he says. "Let's skip the formalities, you can call me Burt. We're scheduled to push off at six, so if you're all game, why don't you follow me over to the marina?"

I nod. I've never been whale watching before. "How long is the tour?" I ask.

"It'll be late. We can make a night of it and have dinner afterwards on the wharf."

I nod. As long as I'm home at midnight to feel Alexander's energy when he sends it to me, I'll be happy. I haven't been able to stop thinking about it all day—along with his letter and the picture. I'm feeling hopeful again.

"Sounds great," Justin and Alenna say, and we all climb into our respective cars and head to the marina.

The firm's yacht is large and luxurious. Mr. Fields (Burt, I guess I should call him), shows us a deck box full of rain ponchos for protection if the ocean spray gets heavy and life jackets if we want them.

"I'll go up to see the captain and tell him we're all aboard," says Burt. "We want as much time to see the whales as possible before we head back for dinner."

I nod. I'm actually kind of excited. This is going to be fun.

We travel far out into Monterey Bay, and the sea life is incredible. In addition to at least five gray whales, we see dolphins, sea lions, otters, and even a sea turtle and jellyfish. As our time is ending I spot a shark cutting smoothly through the water and it reminds me how vast and lawless the ocean is. Way out here in these depths it's just a giant food chain. Survival of the fittest.

"Are we ready to head back?" I ask as we sit on deck, looking out to sea.

"Why don't we wait and watch the sunset?" Burt says. "We don't have to head back just yet."

Justin and Alenna both nod. "It's beautiful out here," she says.

I nod, too, agreeable to whatever they suggest. It's nice to be out in the open ocean, away from the world. I try to tap into the energy that Alexander says he feels out on the ocean but I'm having a little trouble. In the outer reaches of my mind something doesn't feel quite right, but I push those thoughts aside. Alenna's here to protect me.

The sunset is more than worth the wait and as it dips below the horizon, I turn to Burt to thank him once again for asking us to join him. It turned out be a nice day all around, and when I get home I have one more thing to look forward to—Alexander's energy at midnight. I've missed how it feels when we're together.

When it's time to head back, Justin and Alenna head down into the cabin to throw away our empty drink cans and Burt asks me to help him secure the deck. I do as he asks but I'm looking forward to joining Alenna and Justin down in the cabin. It's windy and colder now that it's dark.

"Did you show those files to your mom, Declan?" asks Burt from behind me.

I turn around. "What?"

"Those files you said you found in your attic," he asks.

"Oh," I say, finally understanding what he means. "They're just a bunch of files, and some spreadsheets … oh, and a ledger, too. I haven't had a chance to look at them in detail yet. I will, though, before I bring them in so I can scan and file them properly."

"Has anyone else seen them?" he asks.

The hairs on the back of my neck stand up. *Why is he asking me this?* "No," I say. "Just me."

He nods. "That's good. We had some trouble with Marty a while back. Some of the estates he handled. We sorted it out though."

He must mean Martin Morris, his old partner. "I don't think the files I have are what you're looking for then," I say. "I looked through them a bit, and all of the estates in my dad's files were ones you handled."

Burt's expression changes and immediately I feel the energy shift between us. Something in his eyes makes me realize my folly almost the second the words are out my mouth. "I'll just throw them out," I say quickly, swallowing hard. "I'm sure they're unimportant."

Burt stares at me for a long beat and I can see he's deliberating. I can also see in his eyes when he's made his decision. He releases a heavy sigh.

"I think it's too late for that now, Declan," he says.

His voice is hard, with a hint of reluctance.

But perhaps it's not reluctance. Something in his eyes is making my blood run cold because I sense *annoyance*— annoyance at having to tie up a very unfortunate loose end.

Chapter Thirty-Seven

"What do you mean?" I ask Burt, swallowing nervously.

"You're smart, Declan, and detail oriented, just like Frank was," he says with irritation. "I should have known the apple doesn't fall far from the tree."

I glance over at the closed door to the cabin below. I need to get Alenna's attention.

"You'll figure it out eventually, the same way your father did," he says with disdain. "Your father … with his *perfect morals.* I'm going to take a wild guess and say the apple didn't fall far from the tree in that respect, either."

I stare at him with mounting horror and disbelief.

"He was going to tell Marty that I'd been skimming from the estates we managed," he continues. "It started with small amounts, on estates with distant heirs who didn't know any better. And then, as we got a reputation for estate planning and management, I realized no one was looking, why not go for more? How do you think I saved the firm? I had no other choice. I had to do it."

"You *stole* the money to save the firm?"

"I tried to explain it to your father," Burt says. "I told him that with all the pro bono work he insisted on doing I was just taking my fair share of the extra profits we should have been making. But, unfortunately, he didn't choose to understand."

"My dad went without a salary for a year!" I say with disgust as the realization sinks in. "And you were embezzling money from the clients the whole time?"

"I couldn't very well make the problems disappear overnight," he says. "That would have raised suspicions."

"Is that how you paid for all your houses?" I spit out. "And your cars? And all those vacations?"

"Declan," he says, "you're not factoring in that the scandal would have hurt the firm. It wasn't just me I was protecting. It was everyone who works there. All of our employees." He pauses, his words dripping with condescension. "You're young and you probably don't understand, but you have to be practical about these things."

I stare at him, incredulous. "How long has this been going on?"

He shakes his head. "We don't need to go into any more details. I honestly regret, Declan, that it's come to this." He takes a deep breath. "But I just don't see any other way." He pauses and his expression changes. "I'll tell you the same thing I told Frank, though: It's nothing personal."

The enormity of what he just said hits me with physical force. My knees start to buckle and I grab onto the edge of the deck to remain standing. "What did you say?" I ask with mounting horror.

"We fought," Burt says. "I could tell you it was an accident, but I'm not entirely sure that's true … it actually feels good to finally tell the truth, believe it or not."

"Alenna!" I yell out in horror and panic, but the sound is lost to the gusts of wind ramping up all around us. "Justin!" I cry out, trying again.

"Frank hit his head," Burt continues, "and I had a decision to make …. Ultimately, I decided it was best for everyone if he took his secrets with him into the ocean."

"You threw him overboard?" the words emerge in a croaked whisper as the mounting horror of what he said sinks in. "You're a *monster*," I manage to say, still in a whisper, as the repugnance of his confession raises bile into my throat. I try to sidle closer to the cabin as I keep him in my line of sight.

"Actually," he says, "someone wise once told me there are no monsters. There are just two ways of looking at every situation, and what you see depends on which side you're standing."

I make a dash for the cabin and yell for Alenna at the top of my lungs. He lunges and knocks me down, causing me to hit my head on the deck box. I'm stunned for a second and when I come to, his arms are under my armpits, lifting me up and trying to throw me overboard. I scream for Alenna again and manage to throw my head back and connect with his chin. His grip weakens and I pull free and turn around. He lunges forward to knock me overboard and in that moment I remember a move we learned in aikido. *Use your opponent's energy against them.* I twist my upper body to the side at the last moment and use my planted foot and my lower center of gravity to guide his momentum past me with my arms. He tumbles face first over the side and into the open water. In that moment, the cabin door opens and Alenna pokes her head out. "You guys coming in or what?" she asks.

"Alenna!" I say, chest heaving with adrenaline, "Burt just attacked me! He confessed that he killed my dad! I pushed him overboard."

"*What?*" she says, running up to the deck. "Where is he?"

I point to the water where I can hear him yelling for help as he dips below the cresting waves. "Where are the life preservers?" I ask as I search around the deck in a panic.

She grabs a life preserver from the deck box and throws it out to him and when Burt swims to it, she starts to pull him in.

Just then I see a figure in a captain's hat emerge from the direction of the bridge. He must have heard the commotion and he's coming to help. As he gets closer, my relief turns to horror. All the air rushes from my lungs as I realize now why we haven't seen the captain our entire trip.

Because he's not a captain. Not really.

He's Avestan.

Chapter Thirty-Eight

The look of horror and surprise on my face must be thoroughly amusing to him. He saunters towards us with the same satisfied smile he flashed when he saw me tending Zeno in the street.

I need to warn Alenna.

"It's Avestan!" I shout. "Behind you!"

She turns her head just as Avestan reaches her and I freeze in terror. What happens next makes my blood pool and I can't feel my extremities.

Avestan wraps his arms around Alenna's waist from behind and kisses her neck. "Hey, baby," he purrs, his voice deep and silky.

As I try to grasp what my oxygen-starved brain is telling me I'm seeing, Alenna turns in his arms and kisses him back. Passionately.

When they finish Alenna turns to me. "Surprise," she says mockingly.

"I don't understand …" I say, stuttering to get the words out.

"I began to see things clearly after you came along," she says bitterly. "Little by little I realized what was in front of me. Avestan is the one who always loved me. Before and now. Not like Alexander who changed his mind."

I hear her words but I can't believe them. She's with Avestan? For how long? Has she been fooling me, and hating me, from the start?

"I loved you enough to kill for you," Avestan says as he tugs her close with his arm around her waist. "And I'll do it again," he says.

"But he killed *you*, Alenna," I shout over the wind.

"I couldn't let anyone else have her," Avestan says to me. Then he turns to Alenna and kisses her again. "That's how much I loved you."

"I became a guardian, Declan," Alenna says to me dismissively. "That's hardly killing me."

"And now we can be together forever," says Avestan, pulling her close against him.

I'm sickened by their twisted logic. "He didn't know you'd be a guardian when he killed you, Alenna. And now you're a *fallen* guardian. The worst kind."

"Is it?" says Avestan. "I personally think they're the most interesting kind of guardian. And it's amusing you feel that way, considering."

Alenna lowers the ladder to Burt in the ocean and he climbs back into the boat. I assume they're going to let him at me all over again but Avestan does something unexpected. He ties Burt's hands behind him with a rope. Then he ties his ankles together, too. When Burt starts to complain Avestan raises his hand and a bolt of black light hits Burt in the chest, shocking him into submission. "You're useless," Avestan says to him with contempt as he kicks Burt's legs out from under him, causing him to land on the deck at Avestan's feet.

"Alenna," Avestan calls out to her. "Bring out Justin now. Let's make this interesting."

Alenna goes into the cabin and emerges carrying Justin's limp body. My heart sinks to the ground. *Justin.*

She tosses him onto the deck and Avestan turns to me. "He's not dead," Avestan says. "Not yet, anyway."

"Justin!" I call to him but he lays still, lifeless.

"I'm going to give you a choice," Avestan says. "To show you how malleable the concepts of right and wrong are. Even for someone like yourself. You have a choice to save one life and one life only. If you push Burt overboard," he says, lifting Burt to a standing position and propping him up against the edge of the deck, "with his hands and feet tied, you save Justin. If you choose not to push Burt over, I kill Justin. It's that simple."

I look at Alenna. "You can't let him do this," I say.

"You already pushed him overboard once," Avestan says. "What's the harm in doing it again?"

"I was defending myself from him trying to kill me!" I shout back.

"But wouldn't that be a *just* ending?" he asks. "To push him overboard in cold blood? Since he killed your father? An eye for an eye and all that?"

I look at Alenna again. "How can you do this?"

"It's a choice, Declan," Avestan continues. "Who will you kill? The man who just told you he murdered your own father? Or your innocent friend here, Justin? The choice seems obvious. It's amazing how easy killing can be when you're placed in the right circumstances."

"Don't do it, Declan," Burt says to me with fear in his eyes. "They made me do it."

"That's a good point, Burt," Avestan says with dry ridicule. "Let's make sure Declan knows exactly what that means, so she can make a fully informed decision." He turns to me. "What if I told you that Burt here was *influenced* to do what he did?" He looks at Burt mockingly. "What if I told you he's just a good man who was in a tight spot and he listened to the supposedly wrong voices to earn himself lavish rewards? And what if I told you he did it not just once, but over and over and over again, didn't you Burt? You liked the tasted of it," he says, staring into Burt's panicked, frightened eyes before he turns back to me. "Remember the connection I told you we share, Declan? It has two very interesting, intersecting parts … the first part, which I'll tell you now, is that my Maker was the one who influenced Burt all those years ago. He's the one who tipped the first domino that led to your father's death. Does that make it easier or harder to push Burt over and let him die out there in the ocean?"

The anger burning in my stomach is raw and without end. I feel it raging in my core and I survey the situation, seemingly in slow motion. Burt, sickening as he is, pleading with his eyes for his life; Justin laying lifeless with Avestan standing over him.

"The train is barreling down the tracks, Declan. Not making a decision is a decision of its own," Avestan says. He raises his hand to direct a bolt of energy toward Justin and in that moment, furious rage swells within me. Avestan's evil has hurt me and the people I love for the last time. I feel the burning light within my core surge with the fury in my heart and I thrust out my hand in front of me, releasing a white hot flash of light that bursts out like a cannonball and strikes Avestan in the chest, knocking him back, hard, before he can harm Justin. I fall forward to my knees from the momentum and land next to Justin, who I can now confirm with relief is alive. He's groaning but not moving.

The last thing I remember is looking up at Alenna before something hard hits my head and the water swallows me whole.

Chapter Thirty-Nine

I'm drifting. Bobbing in the waves as my arms and legs move back and forth languidly with the current to keep me afloat. *Where am I? What am I doing here?*

I look around in the dark, confused, but I can barely see past the waves and the ocean that extends in all directions. Slowly, slowly, the icy water revives me fully and I remember how I ended up here. I look around but there's no boat in sight. I touch the back of my head where it hurts and feel sticky wetness.

I'm tired.

So tired.

I shake my head to clear it. *Don't give in, Declan.* I attempt to float on my back to conserve energy but it's difficult as I get tossed in the crests and valleys of the swells. I search for the North Star in the sky above me. Isn't that how ancient explorers found their way? I need something, anything, to indicate which direction to swim. I think I locate it but I'm unsure. *Why didn't I pay more attention when Finn was always pointing things out in the sky?* If only Finn could help me now. Sweet, steadfast Finn. He'd know exactly which direction to go. I want to cry but I can't let myself. *Man up, Jane!* shouts my inner drill sergeant. I need her now more than ever. "Trust your instincts," I hear Alexander whisper in my mind. But didn't Alenna say the same thing? And look where that got me? I never realized she was working against me, possibly the whole time.

You knew, but you didn't trust it. That's true. I felt something was wrong on the boat. If I paid closer attention I would have realized it was a warning. Instead I rationalized it and pushed the thoughts aside.

Not trusting my instincts is what got me here.

I need to trust them now.

I force myself to concentrate the way Alexander taught me. I struggle to find my light in the center of my body. I look up into the sky and find the North Star. Then I get my bearings and start swimming. "Trust yourself," I say out loud to firmly secure the thought in my brain. *You're going the right way,* I hear a voice whisper back. *Did I really just hear that?* I worry that I'm becoming delirious but I have no choice except to continue to move. If it's humanly possible to swim back to shore I'm going to try. I can't give up.

I swim for what feels like hours and I have no idea if I'm making headway in the right direction. The waves keep coming and I keep swimming but I'm losing steam and the water is starting to feel warm, which I remember is a bad thing, according to a survival show Liz and I watched once. I try to warm myself with the light in my core but whether it's my head injury or hypothermia, I can't think clearly for long enough to fight against it. I'm in the middle of the ocean, helpless and alone. The memory of the shark I saw earlier pops into my head for a brief second but for some reason I don't feel fearful, just accepting. Part of the food chain … the natural order of things.

I feel myself melting into the sea, where I belong. I'm folding into a warm, welcoming blanket that I want to immerse myself in fully so I can stop this endless effort, endless struggle, getting nowhere.

Why keep fighting against the inevitable?

This is how it ends. No more pain. No more worry. Wherever Alexander is, he won't have to put himself in danger for me anymore.

Gradually I cease swaying my arms and legs in the waves and let my body flow beneath the sea, drifting downward, ever deeper … quietly and peacefully … into the abyss.

Avestan has finally won.

A familiar voice breaks through the haze, causing me to open my eyes. *"No!"* it shouts. *"Fight! Declan."*

The shock brings me back to clarity for a moment and I manage to kick to the surface one more time. I gasp for air as I shoot up among the waves.

"Dad?" I say aloud, as I look all around me, tears in my eyes.

I look out over the empty waves and realize that delirium must be playing painful tricks on me. I want to let go in peace. Why is my dad urging me to fight rather than welcoming me with open arms? *Please just let me go.* I'm too tired now … and I just want to Let. Go. I lay back, floating, and allow myself to drift without any effort.

"It's not your time, Declan," I hear my dad's voice whisper to me once again. *"You're almost there."* In a dream I feel my dad's embrace, lifting me along the ocean currents, pointing me towards shore. I relax into his arms and imagine this is what it feels like to cross over. I'm so at peace and the love I feel from my dad is overwhelming. "I love you, dad," I say through tears as I float among the peaks and valleys in his arms. "I missed you so much."

Eventually a wave crashes over me, and then another, churning me beneath the surface, but this time I don't succumb. I rise up spitting and sputtering, fighting again. I haven't let go. I spot the shore in the distance and I start swimming with renewed purpose, remembering why I want to live. To see my mom again. To see Alexander. To see Finn, and Liz. I swim toward land, managing one stroke after another until I'm no longer making headway against the rip current. I swim parallel to shore until, blessedly, finally, I feel the swell taking me in. As my feet touch down to the sandy bottom, a blinding white light tears through the sky and lands on the beach. Alexander runs into the surf and as I collapse into his arms he kisses me, reviving me as we stand in the water, waves crashing around our legs.

"Declan," Alexander chokes out with heavy emotion, "I'm so sorry." He gathers me in his arms and carries me to shore, away from the water.

I can't speak. My emotions are so raw and close to the surface. I bury my head in his shoulder as I hold him tighter. *Is this a dream?*

We reach the edge of the cliffs and he lays me down and runs his hands over my body slowly, warming me with white, healing light.

"Is this real?" I ask weakly.

He nods. "Yes," he chokes out with tears in his eyes. "I'm so sorry, Declan. I didn't know."

"Justin," I say. "And Burt. And Alenna … and Avestan."

"I know," he says. "Justin's safe. Edwin has him."

"How did you find me?" I ask.

"I sent you my energy at midnight like I promised but I could tell you weren't there to receive it and I felt something was wrong."

"Alenna," I say, my voice drifting off.

"I didn't know until it was too late," he says, his voice filled with anguish.

"It wasn't too late," I whisper. "You saved me." I look up into his deep green eyes that I missed so dearly.

"You saved yourself," he says, choked with emotion. "I always knew you were more powerful than you think."

I shake my head. "It was my da-"

"Shh, shh," Alexander says softly, stroking my face. "Save your energy. Let me heal you."

I nod slowly and he kisses me tenderly on the lips, bathing me in warm, white light. I relax, kissing him back and breathing in the energy I crave like oxygen.

I'm finally safe again, in his arms.

Chapter Forty

I awaken in Alexander's bed in what must be a pair of his sweats and a t-shirt. I stretch and reach out for him next to me but he's not there. Before I have time to wonder where he is, he appears in the doorway with a breakfast tray.

"You're finally up," he says.

"What happened to Justin?" I ask. I have a vague memory of Alexander telling me he was safe, but I'm having a hard time parsing reality from delirium.

"He's fine. Resting at home. Edwin felt it was better that he not remember anything. Justin thinks he went home after work yesterday. He'll have no memory of being on the boat."

"And Burt?" I ask.

Alexander shakes his head. "Gone."

"Do you know what he told me about my dad?" I say, tears welling up as I remember his confession. The thought of my dad dying in that way, knowing his best friend turned against him brings on fresh waves of pain. "And that Malentus was connected to it?"

Alexander sets the tray down and puts his arms around me. "I know everything. Edwin and Alenna had quite a confrontation late last night. I'm so sorry, Declan, that we didn't see what was going on. And the connection."

"Avestan said there were two ways he and I were connected."

"Edwin and I are looking into it. It's hard to tell truth from lies with him."

"Was Alenna working against us from the start?"

He shakes his head. "She's not giving details. When I came back to San Mar and she kissed me it may have been after that … but I never would have suspected she would fall prey to Avestan's evil. I'm sick that I missed it."

I reach over and squeeze his hand. "You weren't here. We all missed it. Edwin, too."

He nods, quiet.

"Alenna said the kiss was staged," I say.

"It was, partially, to let Avestan see us together. But the way Alenna kissed me wasn't, and afterwards, when we were alone and I didn't respond the way she wanted, she was upset."

"So that's why Avestan didn't follow you? Because Alenna was telling him not to?"

"It looks that way."

My mind races over last night's events. "I have to tell Mr. Morris what Burt was doing, stealing from the firm. And I have to tell my mom about my dad. "

"There'll be time for that later. Right now you should rest."

I nuzzle against him, marveling at the fact that I'm truly here, with Alexander. "I'm not tired, actually," I say with surprise. "Why do I feel so good?"

He smiles. "I may have given you a little extra light energy, to make sure you healed fully."

"Is that what this is?" I say, stretching out my legs and arms, amazed at how energized I feel. "You can do that to me anytime."

"So are you hungry?" he asks.

I nod, realizing that I'm ravenous.

"Your favorite veggie omelet and fresh-squeezed orange juice," he says as he sets down the tray in my lap.

I thank him profusely and that's when it hits me. "Oh my God," I say. "I have to call my mom. She must be worried. I was supposed to be home last night."

He holds up his hand. "I already called her. Everything's fine. She knows you're here."

"Did you tell her what happened?"

He looks at me like I'm crazy. "That you were almost killed by dark angels? No. She thinks I just got back into town and you went out with co-workers to dinner on the wharf and met up with me later on your way home. I told her I was calling because you dropped your phone in the water and couldn't. That part's true. I fished your mobile out of the pocket of your jeans and put it in a bowl of rice. Hopefully it'll be okay in a couple days."

"You can heal me, a living, breathing person, but you can't heal a cell phone?"

He smiles. "I don't care as much about a cell phone as I care about you."

I nod. "Give me about five minutes with this omelet and then I have about a million more questions for you."

He laughs again and sits down on the bed beside me. "I'm not leaving your side, so go ahead and eat."

I tuck into my omelet and after eating nearly all of it and draining my juice glass I'm thoroughly sated and I turn to Alexander. "First question: where were you?" I ask. "While you were gone?'

"Far from here in a region of the world perpetually at war."

"You won't tell me exactly?"

"I moved around. I was following Malentus. You can probably guess all the places."

"What happens now?" I ask. "Since Avestan never followed you and the plan didn't work?"

"Part of the plan did work," he says.

"What do you mean?"

"While you were on the boat fighting for your life with Avestan I managed to wound his Maker. Severely."

"You wounded Malentus? How?"

He lifts his shirt to reveal a long, curved scar from below his heart to the lower reaches of his ab muscles.

"Oh my God, Alexander," I say, reaching for him, "are you okay?"

"This won't be going away, but it was worth it. I managed to weaken Avestan, and the rest of Malentus's line. It'll last for a while."

"Is that why I was able to knock Avestan down?"

He shakes his head. "It's not immediate. Don't diminish it. You saved your friend. When your heart's involved you can do anything."

"I thought you said Malentus was too powerful to go after."

He takes a deep breath before answering. "I found out that when *my* heart's involved I'm stronger than I think, too. And everyone has their weakness, if you take the time to find it."

"What was Malentus's weakness?"

"Being cocksure. Your favorite word."

I meet his eyes and see the glint in them. "You're making jokes?"

"It happens to be true."

"You risked your life," I say, my voice cracking. "I didn't want you to do that."

"It gave us more time together."

"How much time?"

"A while."

"So it's not over?" I ask.

"It's delayed."

"Do you have another plan?"

He smiles. "You know that I do. But let's not talk about that now. I just want to enjoy being with you again, safe, for a while."

"So you're more powerful than Avestan now?"

"You're wounding my pride by not assuming that I always was," he says with a grin, putting his hand over his heart. "But that's the hope, yes."

"The *hope?* You better be kidding," I say, pushing his arm, "because joking about something like this isn't funny."

He smiles. "Avestan will go into hiding again. But I'm going to find him this time before he rebuilds his strength."

"Does that mean you're going to leave again?"

He shakes his head. "The last thing I want to do is leave your side again anytime soon. Can we talk about this later? I have something vitally important I need to do."

"What?" I say, concerned.

"Tell you that I love you. And I missed you. Terribly. And I'm going to kiss you. Right now."

I smile into his eyes as he does just that.

Chapter Forty-One

As Alexander and I lay together in companionable silence, I breathe in the intoxicating nearness of him again. The harmony of our energies fills the air and I lie with my head on his chest, listening to the steady metronome of his heart. "Is it possible my dad saved me?" I ask.

Alexander stops stroking my hair for a moment. "Why do you ask?"

I raise my head to look up at him. "I tried to hang on … but then I couldn't anymore and I wanted to let go. But then I heard my dad whisper that it wasn't time. He held me and carried me until I was close enough to shore to swim again. I thought maybe I was delirious but it felt real."

Alexander meets my eyes. "Anything's possible."

"So you think it was him?"

"Sometimes," he says, "when a soul meets a violent end they don't want to let go fully until the truth is revealed."

"You mean they're trapped?"

"No. More like limited in what they can do and where they can go. By their own choosing."

"So you're saying once Burt confessed what really happened, it released my dad?"

"It may have freed him—to expand his choices, and his ability to communicate or move on. But I want you to understand that this is conjecture on my part."

"I don't know if I should tell my mom," I say.

"That your father spoke to you?"

"No, that he was murdered."

"Why?"

"It will only cause her fresh heartache, like it did for me. And Burt drowned at sea, just like my dad, so it feels as if cosmic justice has been paid." I look up at him. "How is that going to be explained by the way?"

"As far as anyone will ever know, he was out on his boat alone and had an accident at sea."

I nod, remembering his final moments, filled with desperation and fear, and my stomach feels sick again. That's how my dad must have felt, too. "I'll make sure he's exposed for cheating the firm so people can get paid back," I say, "but what good would it do to dredge up my dad's death again? When there's nothing that can be done? Except make my mom hurt even worse, knowing my dad died violently and was betrayed by his best friend?"

Alexander nods. "Why don't you take some time to think about it," he says quietly.

I nod and he takes me in his arms and we lay back, my head on his chest.

We stay like that for a long time, quiet and contemplative, and enjoying the feeling of being in each other's arms again, our energies humming in harmony, where we belong.

Chapter Forty-Two

"You're sure we don't need protection?" Alexander is driving us, finally, to what I've been waiting for and honestly wondered if would ever actually happen. Our plan. Tonight. I'm nervous and excited and profoundly curious about where we're going.

"Guardians can't extend the line in that way," Alexander says. "And it probably goes without saying but I'm fully clean, health-wise."

I smile. "Are there any angels walking around out there with STDs?"

He glances over. "No," he says, with a grin that reaches his eyes.

"Where are you driving us?"

"You honestly think I would ruin it now after we've waited this long?"

"No," I laugh, "but I was starting to think this would never happen.

"There's a time and a place for everything," he says with a smile. "And this is finally our time and our place, again."

He reaches over and takes my hand in his and I grin and face forward in the car as we continue to drive. My insides are tingling I'm so excited.

"You're sure you want to do this?" he asks. "We can wait if you want to."

I look over at him. "Now you're just messing with me."

He laughs. "Just making sure."

He turns onto a familiar road.

"We're going up to the mountains?" I'm excited because this is what I hoped.

"Yes," he says, "and no ... at first."

We bump along the gravel access road in the back of Redwood Park until he stops the car where we normally hike in and opens my door for me to get out.

"We don't have to carry anything?" I ask, looking in the back of his Jeep for any food or supplies.

"It's all there already." Then he pauses and trails his eyes over me. "You look beautiful," he says with a measure of awe.

I smile. I'm wearing the same blue dress I wore when we first kissed. I consider it supremely lucky and I haven't worn it since that night.

"So do you," I say, admiring his tall frame in his dark suit and crisp white shirt in the dusky final light of the evening. He's honestly so handsome with his thick, dark hair, deep green eyes, and the way he carries himself so confidently, that the only way I can describe how I'm feeling right now would be *highly swoony.* "I feel very lucky," I say.

"I'm the lucky one," he says as he takes my hand with a look in his eyes that makes my stomach clench.

I start to walk in the direction of our favorite place.

"That's not where we're going," he says, gently pulling me back.

"We're not?"

"No," he says, "not yet. I have a confession to make."

"What?" I ask tentatively, not sure where this is going.

"I didn't have this as part of the plan at first."

"You didn't ..."

He shakes his head. "But then that day that we were up on the mountain and you said it would be the perfect spot, it got me thinking."

"And?"

"And I realized that maybe it should be the plan. Maybe I was making the plan too complicated."

"So you changed the plan?"

He smiles and shakes his head once more. "But then I thought, I came up with this plan for a reason. Because of something else you once said, and there are some things I want you to see. Things I want to share with you."

"So you didn't change the plan ..."

"I *added* to the plan," he says with a smile. "In the spirit of anticipation."

"I'm definitely feeling the anticipation," I say and he laughs.

"We're going to travel by light," he says "and I'll explain more when we get there, but I want you to know that eventually we're going to end up here. In the spot you said would be perfect."

I nod, smiling, a happy lump in my throat. "I love your plan already," I say. "I don't even know what it is, but I love it."

He smiles. "Come here," he says, his voice low and husky as he pulls me closer. My knees go weak at the look in his eyes as he stares down at me.

He lets go of my hands and wraps his arms around me, pulling me tight against him, and he bends down to kiss me. As I lose myself in the sensation of his lips on mine, I feel us transform into pure light energy and as we take flight and soar into the sky, everything becomes a blur as we travel faster than we've ever flown before. The feeling is pure joy and thrilling excitement, as if we're one being, joined in a vibration of light energy, and I surrender to the state of complete and utter bliss.

Before long we land high on a mountain, in daylight, and as we become solid, Alexander kisses me again, softly. We stare into each other's eyes, enjoying the after-sensation of flying together, and then we turn and look at the view. "I dreamed of coming here with you," he says.

I look out over an expanse of lush green mountains and sheer cliffs of red rock leading down into a secluded cove, far below, with the most brilliantly blue-green water I've ever seen. A long, free-falling waterfall flows from the top of the mountain, over the cliff face and down into the deep, vibrant azure pool below. I've never seen anything more breathtaking and beautiful. I recognize the beautiful sight before me from descriptions he's shared with me many times. "Are we in Australia?" I ask, amazed and awe-struck.

He nods. "You said you wanted to come here with me. It's one of my favorite places in the world and I wanted to share it with you. And I wanted to make our first time here together especially memorable."

I turn to look at him, eyes welling up with emotion. "It's beautiful," I say, my voice cracking. "More beautiful than I even imagined from your descriptions."

He smiles. "Would you like to go down and swim under the waterfall?"

"Can we?"

"You're with an angel—we can do anything we want."

I smile. "You don't have to impress me, you know. I already fell for you, hopelessly, a long time ago."

He laughs. "What's the point of being an angel if you don't chuck your brass about once in a while to impress your girlfriend?"

He takes me in his arms and we fly, by light, until suddenly we're at the base of the cove, standing on some rocky sand near that beautiful azure water. "What's this?" I ask, pointing to a cooler and a picnic blanket spread out on the ground.

"That's for us. I was here earlier getting it ready."

I smile. I really do love his plans. "What do we do for swimsuits?" I ask.

"We don't need them."

"What if someone comes?"

"This place is difficult to get to. I promise you, we won't run into anyone."

I nod.

"Is that okay with you? I can get some if you prefer."

I shake my head. "No, I like this idea."

He smiles. "Do you want to hear the rules?"

"*Rules?*"

"To build anticipation. For later."

I'm intrigued. "Okay."

"First rule: We strip. Slowly."

I smile. "Is that it?"

He shakes his head, a wicked glint in his eyes. "There's more."

"Tell me."

"Then we get into the water and we swim for the waterfall."

"Okay."

"We can kiss," he says, his voice low, "and *touch* … any time you want, but there's one rule that's essential."

My eyebrow rises. "And that is?"

"We can't make love."

"I thought that was the whole reason we came here."

"Not yet," he says. "That's for later."

"In San Mar?"

"Yes. In the spot you said would be perfect." And then he adds, "If you're amenable."

"Oh, I'm amenable all right," I say with a smile.

He laughs. "I thought so."

"So should we start?" I ask.

"There's one more thing."

I laugh. "This plan is pretty elaborate."

"I've thought about it a lot."

"I'm sure you have," I say with a smile.

"There are limits to where we can touch," he says, "for now, with our hands."

He meets my eyes and we both smile. "Let me guess, that would be the parts that would be covered up with bathing suits? If we had them?"

"I was going to say elbows," he says, "but your plan sounds better."

I laugh. "Let me make sure I'm clear on these rules of yours. We're not allowed to touch each other with our *hands* in those places ... but what if we were kissing and you happened to lift me up and I wrapped my legs around you?"

His eyes go dark. "That could be dangerous," he says, his voice low. "But, as I think you know, I'm not afraid of danger."

I smile. "And I imagine you're also not afraid of creativity."

His eyebrow rises. "Creativity is encouraged," he says with a gleam in his eyes. "For both of us. I have some eminently creative ideas planned myself."

I swallow hard as my heart beats faster. "You go first," I say.

He smiles and starts by taking off his suit jacket. I follow by removing my necklace.

"Cheater," he says and I laugh.

He unbuttons his shirt, slowly, and removes it. The muscles of his chest are smooth and sculpted and I see the long, curved scar left by Malentus which reaches down to where his pants hang low on his hips. Seeing the scar takes me out of the moment for a brief second but I swallow hard at the sight of the low "v" of his abs and his smoldering eyes. I turn around so he can unzip my dress and then I turn back around and let it fall to the ground, leaving me in just my bra, panties and heels. He takes a deep breath and unbuckles his pants and removes them, along with his socks, and places them alongside his shirt and jacket. Now he's left in just his boxer briefs. I step out of my heels and unclasp my new lacy blue bra, letting it fall to my feet. Alexander's appreciation, and interest, is evident. "You're so beautiful," he says, his voice low. His eyes trace a path over and around the outlines of my body. I start to remove my panties, slowly, and he slides down his boxer briefs with equal patience until we're both left standing before each other, magnificently naked. His eyes are dark and wanting and Alexander's energy is full of love—along with a very un-angel-y desire, which I also like—and it all combines to make me feel confident and beautiful rather than self-conscious in any way. Being with him, like this, feels natural … and right. "You have no idea how beautiful you are," he breathes. I feel my stomach clench, way down low, at the sight of him. He reaches out his hand to take mine and we walk slowly into the azure pool. I revel in the way the water feels as it rises over my bare skin, every nerve-ending charged with delicious, electric anticipation.

We swim over to the waterfall and he pulls me closer under the cascading spray and kisses me for the first time in our private, stunningly-beautiful oasis. Our hands roam, within the limits we've set forth, and when I wrap my legs around him in the water he groans softly, deep within his throat, and breathes my name in my ear, "*Declan.*"

Eventually he lifts me up and carries me behind the waterfall where we kiss against the red rock cliffs, water pouring all around us.

And then, with the pounding rush of the waterfall as a backdrop, Alexander shows me how truly creative a guardian can be.

Chapter Forty-Three

"Are you ready for our next stop?"

Alexander and I have been lying on our backs on a large, flat, warm rock in the sun, drying off after our swim. "Our next stop?" I ask. "You mean before we go back to San Mar?" I turn my head to look at him beside me. I don't think I've ever felt so relaxed and content in all my life. Holding hands, lying next to Alexander, has to be one of my favorite things in the world.

"Another treasured spot of mine that we've talked about," he says. "But I want to show you this one at night, so I'm going to have to mess with time a bit, which will take some extra effort."

"Is that why you're doing all this?" I ask, "To weaken yourself ... for us, later?"

He shakes his head. "I wanted to bring you to these places regardless. The fact that it will tire me out is a bonus."

I squint in the sun, shading my eyes with my hand. "I don't know if I like the fact that you have to tire yourself out to be with me."

"But I'm looking forward to tiring myself out with you. Many times."

I smile. "I'm serious."

"So am I. It feels good to expend energy and just focus on relaxing, and feeling, and *being* with you."

I take a deep breath and close my eyes for a moment. "I love the way I feel when we're together," I say. "I feel calm and serene—and electrified—all at the same time. I hope that's how you feel with me."

He looks over and meets my eyes. "Remember when I told you how I like to be out on the ocean? Away from mortals and just quiet in nature? Peaceful?"

I nod.

"That's how you make me feel," he says as he leans over and kisses me. "All the time. You're my oasis from the storm of the world. And you make my every molecule stand at attention."

I smile and turn on my side to face him and he does the same, pulling me closer and kissing me softly again.

"So you're ready to go?" he murmurs as he trails kisses along my jaw and neck.

"I could stay here forever," I murmur back, reveling in his kisses and the heat of his breath in my ear.

"Me, too, but you're going to like our next stop. I promise."

We kiss a while longer and then we sit up and he hands me my clothes, which have been perfectly warmed in the sun. We both get dressed leisurely and then we stand before one another and he takes me in his embrace and kisses me softly. We're off again, shooting up to the sky as we transform into light energy and immerse ourselves in total bliss again. My chest swells from all the love in my heart as we travel together, as one entity, rocketing through bright blue skies until we reach the night.

We soar over an island and land up high and, as we transform into solid matter again, I look around to see that we're up on a hill overlooking a gorgeous beach below, lit by starlight. I can hear the waves breaking rhythmically and lapping against the shore. As beautiful as it is, I'm compelled to look up to the night sky above us. It's remarkably clear and brilliant, like nothing I've ever seen.

"This is one of my favorite places to see the stars," Alexander says. "I wanted you to see the universe with me, from here."

I smile as he looks over at me. Again, I see that Alexander has planned ahead. Lying on the ground next to us is a large picnic blanket, with another blanket folded and ready to keep us warm if we need it. There's also another cooler with two thermoses beside it. We sit down and he hands me one of the thermoses. "Hot chocolate," he says.

"You think of everything," I say with a smile as I take a sip. I close my eyes to savor it for a moment. It's delicious.

"Still annoyed by my planning?" he asks.

I push his arm. "I love your plans. I *adore* your plans. I was only annoyed when you didn't tell me you *had* a plan. For *us*."

He smiles and kisses me. "I have a lot of plans for us."

"What else is in the cooler?" I ask.

"Are you hungry?"

"No, just curious. I'm still full from our last stop."

He smiles. "I have more fruit and some of those granola bars you like. Here's a torch if you want to take a look." He passes me a flashlight and I flick it on to illuminate the inside of the cooler. Then I turn it off. It's more peaceful in the dark.

"Who cleans all this up after we leave?"

"I do," he says, "tomorrow. There's no rush."

I nod.

"I'm glad you're always looking out for the maintenance of a pristine wilderness," he says.

I push his arm. "I'm just curious, that's all. I like to know the mechanics of how you angels do what you do."

He laughs. "I wasn't putting you on. I like that about you … that you worry about the details."

I lean over and plant a kiss on his lips. Then I sit back and take in all the beauty around us, from the sound of the ocean lapping against the shore below, to the star-saturated sky above us. "This is incredible," I say, awe-struck for the second time today. "What is that?" I ask, pointing to a beautiful swath of stars and light stretching across the sky. I've never seen anything like it—it's as if a painter used stars instead of paint to smear a sweeping diffusion of light above us.

"Lean back," he says and we both set our thermoses down and lie on our backs next to each other on the picnic blanket, pulling the other blanket over us for warmth. He reaches for my hand, as he always does. His hand is large and warm and I love the feel of his fingers threaded through mine.

"That's the Milky Way," he says, pointing to the swath of stars and light with his free hand. And those two patches of glowing light," he says as he points over to the right, "are the greater and lesser Magellanic Clouds."

"It's amazing," I breathe. We sit silent for long minutes, absorbing the awesome beauty before us. "It makes me feel very small," I say softly, "and connected. To everything."

He turns his head and meets my eyes. "I knew you'd get it."

He holds my gaze and reaches over to pull me close. "And now, Miss Jane, I'm going to kiss you under these stars, for quite a while … if you're amenable, that is."

I smile. "Oh, I'm amenable, Mr. Ronin. Do the same rules apply?"

"Yes," he laughs, "and I must warn you that I plan to get exceptionally creative again."

"You're very gifted in the creativity department."

"As are you," he says with a mischievous smile, "truly inspiring."

I laugh as he draws the blanket over us some more and then pulls me in for a long, slow kiss.

And then, under the ornament of the Milky Way and the vast expanse of stars in the universe, we explore together how deeply inventive we can be.

Chapter Forty-Four

"Maybe we should call it a night," Alexander says as we lie still, holding hands, looking up at the stars.

I nudge against him. "Very funny."

"What do you think of my plan so far?" he asks, turning his head to look at me.

I hold his gaze for a moment before answering. "I know you're expecting me to make a joke here but my heart feels so full right now, I don't think I can." Tears well up in my eyes. "This has all been so beautiful. And perfect. I love your plan. And I love *you*. More than I can express in words."

He squeezes my hand and rolls over to kiss my lips softly. "It's not too much?"

I shake my head. "Not at all. Although I have to say, you've taken anticipation to greater heights than I ever thought possible."

He laughs. "I'm a firm believer in the power of a slow build."

"Anticipation makes it sweeter," I say with a smile. "You've proven that, many times."

He leans over and kisses me again.

"I don't know why but I'm feeling a little nervous," I say.

"You are? Do you want to stop?"

"No, not at all. It's just that I've been looking forward to this for so long and this night has been so perfect and we're both, obviously, more than ready … but I just don't want it to be a letdown when we get back to San Mar … and finally stop with the rules ...”

His eyes show compassion. “Declan,” he says, stroking my cheek “we could never let each other down. Even if the night stopped here, it already outstrips every sexual encounter I've ever had.”

I smile, my mortal heart swollen to outsize proportions.

“I love you,” he says, holding my gaze. “We're going to take this slow … and we can stop at any time. It's all about communication. We tell each other what feels good. With words and sounds. The same way we've been doing all night.”

I nod. “I love you,” I say softly.

“Are you ready to go to our perfect spot?”

I nod and we kiss and as we lie together under the stars, Alexander transforms us until we're soaring as light back to San Mar.

We land in our space on the mountain, facing out to the stunning beauty spread out like a painting before us. It's still dusk, as if we never left, and the view out over the trees to the ocean in the distance is seared with color. Pink and orange streak through the blue sky as the sun sets over glistening water. We stand, with our arms around one another, appreciating the splendor.

When we turn around, I gasp at the sight before me. There's a small cabin with golden light flickering through the window, erected in the spot where we usually lay our picnic blanket.

I turn to Alexander with my mouth agape. “How did you—?”

“I've been busy,” he says. “And don't worry, the park is closed and I know you're going to ask but I can take it all down and cart it away later, in minutes.”

I laugh. "I wasn't going to ask."

"Yes you were."

"All right," I admit, "I was."

He laughs. "I thought we'd watch the sunset and then go inside."

"That sounds perfect."

He goes into the cabin and returns with a picnic blanket that he unfurls on the ground before me. We sit down on the blanket and he pulls me close into his arms. We look out over the sweeping vista as the sky blazes with vibrant hues and the sun makes its last stand, dipping below the horizon. Then Alexander turns and kisses me softly. "Let's go inside," he says, his words filled with promise. He takes my hand and my stomach clenches in anticipation as he leads me to the cabin. When we walk inside, I gasp at what he's done. All along the beams of the open-framed walls are flickering candles. The votive holders are a beautiful array of blue and white frosted glass. I spin around slowly to see that they surround the room, hundreds of them, casting a romantic glow. In the middle of the space is a large, rustic four-poster bed made up with a fluffy white duvet and overstuffed pillows. And on a small table on the side of the bed is a vase filled with delicate blue and white forget-me-nots.

"The colors of your aura continue to inspire me," he says softly.

I meet his eyes and smile, my eyes welling up. Once more I slowly turn to take in the sight all around me and, with heart overflowing, I meet his eyes again and whisper simply, "It's lovely, and perfect." Then I swallow the lump in my throat and add, "Thank you."

He smiles and steps towards me. "No more rules," he says, his voice low and his eyes never leaving mine. He slowly unzips my dress and I let it fall to the floor. I remove his jacket and slowly unbutton his shirt and slide it off his shoulders. When I open his belt and unzip his pants he takes a deep breath and we both smile. He unclasps my bra, gliding it off my shoulders, and slips his hands under my panties at my hips, easing them down slowly. "You're so beautiful," he says, tracing me with his eyes. I slip my hands under his boxer briefs and slide them off, very slowly, and he watches me, eyes dark and molten. He lifts me effortlessly, still holding my gaze, and carries me to the bed where he lays me down and his mouth finds mine. His kiss is soft at first, teasing, and then he parts my lips and the kiss deepens, his tongue stroking mine in a languid, sensuous dance. We kiss and touch, everywhere, and the feeling is beyond exquisite. I moan softly and he answers with low groans from deep within his throat as our hands roam freely, unbound by previous rules. Every nerve is electrified, my whole being in a heightened state of awareness as he kisses every inch of me, slowly, and whispers hot in my ear, "I dreamed of this."

Slowly, he spreads my legs with his knees and glides his desire over my most sensitive area and when I moan at the delicious pleasure he smiles. My body is aching for him, *longing* for him, and when I think I can no longer bear it, he pauses at my entry and looks into my eyes. "You ready?" he breathes, his eyes dark pools of desire. "Yes," I whisper, every nerve ending on fire, wanting him more than anything else in the world. "We'll take it slow," he says, his voice low as he holds my gaze and presses against my entry until I feel him thrust inside. "*Ah,*" I cry out, startled at the fullness. He stops, allowing me to adjust to the feeling of having him inside me. "You okay?" he breathes, his eyes never leaving mine. I nod and he smiles in that way that makes my stomach clench. "I'm going to move now, slowly. Let me know how this feels," he says and then he starts to move, very slowly, as promised, and I gasp at the pleasure. "Good?" he asks. "More than good," I breathe and he smiles back, eyes darkening again with desire. "I love you," he whispers as he pushes in again, deliciously slow, and I marvel at the satisfying fullness. He continues the slow thrusts in and out and when I wrap my legs around him and moan softly his eyes smolder and his mouth comes down on mine. We kiss, softly at first, and then with more urgency, as we continue to make love and I realize that Alexander was right: this is far, far better than I ever could have imagined. A swell of tension builds and concentrates within me, slowly and powerfully, climbing higher and higher as Alexander continues to move, slowly at first and then gradually faster, until I can feel that we're both reaching a flash point of no return. We cry out each other's names as our energies join and detonate in a blazing eruption of brilliant white light, leaving us spent and gasping as waves of intense pleasure roll through me. Alexander grips me tight and collapses on my chest, breathing hard as we ride out the blissful after-effects together. He looks up and meets my eyes.

"I want to say I love you but I can't speak," he says with effort.

I laugh, still catching my breath. "I don't think you've ever been speechless before."

"I've never felt like that before. Did you feel it, too?"

I nod. "Is that how it always is the first time?"

"In a word, no," he says with a laugh. He looks into my eyes and shakes his head. "I should have known."

"Known what?"

"That being with you is a never-ending incredible surprise."

I smile.

"It usually takes time to get better," he explains, "as partners get to know one another and they communicate what they like."

"It's going to get *better?*"

He laughs. "I guess we'll have to find out."

Alexander kisses me, and then we talk, and we kiss and talk some more, and eventually we find out, many times, that, yes, amazingly, it does get better and better when you're with the person you love.

Epilogue

As Alexander holds me in his arms, I begin to drift off to sleep in his warm embrace, wholly content and smiling dreamily.

I watch as the candles glow beautifully along the walls and, as my eyes begin to flutter closed, a soft gust of wind causes the candles to flicker. At the same moment, a forgotten memory washes over me of my father's voice, whispering an urgent message to me when I was out in the ocean, drifting among the swells:

"Protect the baby, Declan. At all costs."

Reader's Note

Thank you for reading! If you'd like to find out how Declan and Alexander's story ends, please turn the page for an excerpt from *Revelation*, the final book in the series, available now.

And thank you in advance for supporting authors and helping other readers by considering leaving an online review on Amazon, Goodreads, and/or your favorite blog/website forum for romance readers. I read all my reviews and they are all sincerely appreciated.

Connect with me on the social media sites below—I love hearing from readers!

A.J. Messenger

I welcome you to visit me and subscribe to my newsletter to be the first to know about upcoming releases.

 ajmessenger.com

 facebook.com/ajmessengerauthor

 @aj_messenger

The Guardian Series

Guardian
(book one)

Fallen
(book two)

Revelation
(book three)

More titles by A.J. Messenger coming soon.

Excerpt from Revelation

Preface

In my dream, if it is a dream, the baby is smiling, with wondrous emerald green eyes and a distinct sparkle.

Finn, Liz, and Chief Stephens are all gathered around as my mom holds the baby in her arms with a depth of love I can feel in my heart.

But why is my mom crying? And why does everyone look so sad?

And where is Alexander?

Revelation: Chapter One

This can't be.

I'm *pregnant?*

I stare at the plus sign on the test in my hand but I still don't quite believe it. Even if it is the seventh test stick I peed on.

It's been six weeks since Alexander took me on our amazing night flight around the world and we made love in our perfect spot in the San Mar Mountains. At first I dismissed the message I remembered from my dad as either a dream or a product of synapses firing in a supremely relaxed state. I mean, *c'mon,* I just made love with an angel, who knows what that can do to a person?

But now, staring at the pregnancy test in my hand, which I purchased on a lark because of a missed period not thinking in a million *years* it would come back positive, I can't help but wonder if my memory of my father's message was real. Alexander said that discovering the truth of what happened could have freed his soul to move on. Maybe he's trying to communicate. And help me. When I think about it, it had to have been my dad who saved me out in the ocean. Otherwise, I honestly can't explain how I made it to shore. And now he's trying to warn me: *Protect the baby. At all costs.*

The baby. Can it really be true that I have a life growing inside me? I place my palm over my stomach and imagine the warm, white light in my core protecting all that's within.

As the shock slowly wears off I smile and imagine the amazingly cute baby Alexander and I would make, but then the reality of the situation breaks through again. I just turned nineteen and I also just started my first year of college two weeks ago. Depending on when exactly this supposedly impossible pregnancy occurred … that would make the baby born before I even complete my first year at UCSM. How is that even going to work? *Sorry professor, I'll have to reschedule my finals because I'll be busy having a baby that day.* I chuckle at my ridiculously pragmatic thoughts and then I whipsaw over to a decidedly panicky feeling in my chest.

But the idea of a baby—*Alexander's* baby—although unexpected, sends such joy through me that I can hardly sit still. I'm meeting him at the beach in an hour to go surfing. I want to tell him but I have no idea how he'll react. He insisted it was impossible for guardians to have babies—they can't extend the line in that way. *Guess angels don't always know everything.*

But what if he's not happy with the news? Or what if this breaks some crazy guardian rule I don't know about? *But how could it break a rule, Declan, if it was supposedly impossible?*

I dismiss all of my meandering worries almost the moment I have them. Alexander has shown me time and again that we talk things through and we're honest with each other. Whatever this means, we'll figure it out together … and he'll be thrilled.

I hope.

Revelation: Chapter Two

"Do you ever wonder," I ask Alexander as we're walking with our surfboards, "why we were drawn together like we were?" We're nearly down all the steps to the beach.

He looks over at me and smiles. "In one of my lives, my parents were very different but they had an especially good connection. I remember when people used to ask my mum how they managed to get on so well she used to smile and say: *'There's no greater mystery than whom we spark to and why.'* I never realized how true that was until I sparked to you."

"You think we're very different?" I ask.

"No," he laughs, "we're actually a lot alike. I've just never sparked to someone the way I sparked to you."

I smile. I like that term *sparked*. It perfectly encapsulates how I felt when I saw Alexander for the first time. And every time I see him, in fact. "Do you think," I ask, "that if two people like us spark together, that something impossible can happen?"

We reach a good spot on the beach and he sets down his backpack and jabs his surfboard into the sand and looks over at me. "Sure," he says, "anything is possible … but I don't understand, where is this going?"

"If anything is possible," I say to him as he's pulling up his wetsuit and maneuvering his arms in, "is it possible I could be pregnant?"

He yanks the long pull tab to zip up the back of his wetsuit and looks at me. "*What?*"

"We've had sex," I say. "A lot."

He smiles wryly. "Yes, if two mortals had sex as often as we have without protection, pregnancy would definitely be on the table. But I'm a guardian, we can't have progeny, it doesn't work that way."

"But what if I *am* pregnant?"

He stares at me for a long beat. "What are you saying?"

I swallow. "I'm saying that I bought seven different pregnancy tests from the drugstore and they all came up positive."

He grabs onto the surfboard in the sand beside him. "Are you serious?"

I smile. "Yes."

"How can that be?" I detect a flash of what looks like fear in his eyes, alarming me. But just as quickly a range of other emotions play over his face until eventually he settles on a very slow, very astounded smile. He walks toward me with surprised, joyful eyes and lifts me into his arms, spinning us around. "You're *pregnant?*"

I nod and he brings me back down so he can plant an exuberant kiss on my lips.

"How?" he asks.

"The usual way, I guess."

He laughs. "This isn't supposed to be possible."

"Maybe it's our spark? Or sprite power?"

He stares at me, still incredulous. "That's amazing," he says, his eyes alight.

"Or *'amazeballs'* as Liz would say," I add.

He laughs. "It's incredible, really," he says again, shaking his head in disbelief. "Are you sure? How far along are you?"

"I don't know yet, but I have a feeling it happened the first night we were together, so it could be six weeks."

He does some swift calculations. "So he would be born in April?"

"Or she."

"Or she," he smiles, "of course."

"Yes, I think so. I'll need to go to the doctor to be certain. I looked it up and April would mean a diamond birthstone. As if that means anything. I think finding out I'm pregnant is turning me a little crazy. I was already looking up names online."

He laughs. "A diamond birthstone is very fitting for your aura," he says, "clear and brilliant." He picks me up and spins us around again. "I can't believe this. We're going to have a baby."

"So you're okay with it?" I ask.

He sets me down and meets my eyes. "*Okay* with it? I'm more than okay with it. I'm amazed … and ecstatic … and delirious." He pulls me close again and plants his lips on mine. "I can't believe this," he says again, shaking his head.

I laugh. He does look quite dazed.

"Have you told anyone else yet?" he asks.

I shake my head. "I thought you should be the first."

He smiles and in the back of my mind I picture myself trying to explain my pregnancy to my mom—I have a feeling her reaction will not be quite as thrilled as Alexander's. Not by a long shot.

"Forget surfing, let's go celebrate," Alexander says, starting to take off his wetsuit.

"Wait," I say, "I actually like the idea of just celebrating out on the water. I like sitting on our boards together and waiting for the waves with you."

He smiles and pulls me into his embrace. "I like waiting for anything with you," he says as he kisses me softly in the late summer sun, the sound of the breaking waves our only audience.

"There's something I haven't told you," I say after we've finished surfing for the day and we're sitting on our towels in our swimsuits warming ourselves in the sun. I glance over at Alexander as he runs his fingers through his wet, tousled hair and leans back on his elbows.

"You're having twins?"

I chuckle. Our feet are next to each other in the warm sand and I nudge his foot and toss some sand at his ankle with my toes. "I could be," I say, "for all we know. But that's not what I'm talking about."

"What is it?" he asks.

My eyes trail over his hard, muscled torso, noting the long, curved scar that starts under his heart and traces down over his ribs and disappears near the end of his ab muscles where his board shorts hang low on his hips. I shiver a little as I think about how Avestan's Maker, Malentus, wounded him so badly.

"It's the reason I think I might have gotten pregnant that first night we were together," I say. "I heard something."

He meets my eyes. "What do you mean?"

"As we were falling asleep that night I had a memory from when I was in the ocean. A memory of hearing my dad's voice telling me to *protect the baby, at all costs.* I thought I imagined it … it didn't even make any sense … but now that I'm pregnant I can't help but wonder if it was real."

Alexander sits up from his reclined position. "It sounds real. And, regardless, your dad is right. Our child will be unlike any other being—not a mortal or a sprite or a guardian but something else, and very powerful."

I consider his words. I like the idea of having an especially mighty baby but I also know what that could mean. "So Avestan will come after us?"

Alexander avoids the question. "Let's talk about that later," he says, "for now let's just enjoy the mind-blowing fact that we're going to be parents. We need to get you an appointment with a doctor to confirm it."

I nod. "And to make sure all's well. But what if the doctor looks in there and it has wings or something," I say. "How the heck will I explain that?"

Alexander laughs. "I don't think that will be a problem, but you do tend to surprise, Miss Jane."

"As do you, Mr. Ronin—the guardian who supposedly couldn't get me pregnant."

He laughs. "Touché. I should have realized that nothing with you is ever impossible."

He leans over and kisses me, softly at first, and then in that way he always does that makes my knees weak and my heart swoon.

End of Chapter Two

Read *Revelation* (the final book in the Guardian Series)
Available now

Made in United States
North Haven, CT
16 February 2022

16165950R00141